GREAT ADVICE FROM LILA FENWICK

GREAT ADVICE FROM LILA FENWICK

Kate McMullan
pictures by Diane de Groat

DIAL BOOKS FOR YOUNG READERS
New York

Published by Dial Books for Young Readers
A Division of NAL Penguin Inc.
2 Park Avenue
New York, New York 10016

Published simultaneously in Canada
by Fitzhenry & Whiteside Limited, Toronto
Text copyright © 1988 by Kate McMullan
Pictures copyright © 1988 by Diane deGroat
All rights reserved
Printed in U.S.A.
First Edition
COBE
2 4 6 8 10 9 7 5 3 1

Library of Congress Cataloging in Publication Data
McMullan, Kate. Great advice from Lila Fenwick.
Summary: Lila and her friend spend two weeks
of the summer between fifth and sixth grade
at a Boy Scout camp, where Lila's father is
camp doctor, having a wonderful time learning
about boys and nature too.
[1. Camps—Fiction.]
I. deGroat, Diane, ill.   II. Title.
PZ7.M47879Gm   1988   [Fic]   87-24513
ISBN 0-8037-0529-8
ISBN 0-8037-0532-8 (lib. bdg.)

In memory of my father

*I am especially thankful to the following
Boy Scouts of America for their consultation
in the preparation of this manuscript:
Mr. Russell J. Hart, Mr. Jim Fox,. Danny Marzollo,
and David Marzollo. I am grateful also to
Dr. Morton Schwimmer and Dr. Lee Anderson
for sharing with me their expertise
regarding bee stings.
—Kate McMullan*

CONTENTS

HOW TO
TALK TO BOYS

I wasn't sure how I felt about being called the Mighty Minnow. I parked my towel between Gayle's and Kelly's in the grassy shade behind the diving board and flopped down to think about it. Coach Nilson had meant it as a compliment. He'd said it this morning during the summer's first swim team practice at the Neighborhood Association Pool (unfortunately known as N.A.P.).

"Terrific backstroke!" he'd called to me. "You're our team's secret weapon, Lila! The Mighty Minnow!"

Mighty was okay. That meant I was a powerful swimmer. Klutz that I can be on land, in the water I'm almost graceful—and speedy. But Minnow! I wasn't that short. In fact, I thought I'd been looking taller lately, and older, more grown up. And I'd just gotten some new specs that the optician said made me look extremely sophisticated.

Kelly nudged me. "Lila!" she whispered.

"What?"

"That's the one."

"The one what?"

"Haven't you heard anything we've been saying?" Kelly wrinkled her freckled nose and gave Gayle a look like she couldn't believe I was so out of it. Then she lifted her lemonade carton ever so slightly in the direction of a boy standing beside the shallow end of the pool. "The one in the blue racing suit. That's the one I want you to work on."

Kelly and Gayle and I stared at what looked to me like the back of a boy. He had a head of blond hair, a neck, two arms, two legs, and what our gym teacher calls a trunk. He was talking to Michael Watson, my oldest friend in the world from our fifth grade class— make that *sixth* grade class, next fall. This back-of-a-boy was taller than Michael, and his back looked older somehow. Maybe he was going into seventh grade. Maybe eighth.

"Work on?"

"Work on one of your famous Great Ideas! For getting him to turn around!" Kelly said impatiently.

Great Ideas. I don't know why, but they seem to pop into my brain right when I need them.

"Yeah." Gayle let her long yellow zigzag hair fall

over part of her face as she whispered, "And then work on a Great Idea for getting him to come over here and start talking to us!"

What was with Gayle, anyway? Six months ago she would have sneered at Kelly for being boy crazy. But not now.

"You guys!" I groaned. "This is too easy for a Great Idea. Just yell to Michael and they'll both come over here."

I put my head down on my towel and just lay there, wondering whether Coach might change my secret weapon name to the Terrific Trout. Or maybe the Daring Dolphin. I had my doubts.

"Hey!" Kelly's urgent whisper interrupted my thoughts. "He's turning around!"

"T.K.O. for sure," Gayle said. "A Total Knock-out."

"You think?" Kelly twisted a strand of her sandy, sun-bleached hair around her finger.

"*Definitely*," Gayle replied.

"He's got freckles," Kelly whispered. "Like mine."

"Nice smile," said Gayle.

"It looks sort of lopsided to me," I told them.

"But in a cute way," said Kelly.

"He's got actual muscles," observed Gayle. "Check his chest."

I checked. He did have muscles, but then any chest would look musclely next to Michael's chest, which was all ribs. At that moment I felt a little pang of love for good old Michael, who always kidded that he was so skinny he had to run around in the shower to get wet!

"Kelly," Gayle whispered, "read those Tips for Talking again."

"Oh, come on!" I said. "Enough is enough!"

But Kelly was already flipping through the pages of the magazine she'd swiped from her older sister, trying to locate the article she'd been reading aloud to us earlier that morning. It was called "How to Talk to Boys."

" 'Tip Number One,' " Kelly read. " 'Think of an excuse to talk to him. *Any* excuse. If you want to make him think you are interested in sports, ask about the score of a baseball game.' "

"What if you don't care what the score of the baseball game was?" I interrupted Kelly. "Are you supposed to ask about it anyway?"

"I think so," said Kelly. Then she read on. " 'If you've never met him, you can say he looks familiar and then talk about where you might have seen each other before. It doesn't really matter *what* you say because this is just a way to begin talking.' "

Even in the midmorning shade of early June, it was getting to be a St. Louis summer—hot and sticky. I wanted to get back into the pool and maybe have a game of Marco Polo or jump-dive, and forget about Tips for Talkers. What did Kelly need Talking Tips for anyway? She was the friendliest person in our class! And Gayle—my big best friend, wrapped up in her white terry cloth robe, which she always wore to cover up her extra pounds when she was out of the pool—Gayle was so smart that she'd done tenth grade math in fifth grade. Did she need some dumb magazine to tell her how to talk to boys? No! And why would you ask a boy what the score of a baseball game was if you didn't really want to know? It sounded pretty whacko to me.

Now Michael and the T.K.O. stranger headed in our direction. As they walked around the back of the diving board, Kelly called out, "Hey, Michael! You swimming in the meet on Saturday?"

Michael stopped. "Yeah!" He looked confused. "You heard Coach at practice. I'm doing freestyle. Why?"

"Oh, I just wondered." Kelly smiled at Michael and then at the boy next to him. "How about you?" she asked him. "You swimming for N.A.P. this year?"

Kelly definitely did not need Talking Tips.

T.K.O. shook his head no. "I'm signed up to be a counselor this summer," he said, "but when I do swim, it's for Shaw Park."

You have to be a really great swimmer just to make it onto the Shaw Park team. Not like N.A.P. If you can breathe, you can swim for N.A.P. Then T.K.O. grinned a crooked grin and added, "Anyway, I wouldn't swim for this sleepy team!"

"Hey!" objected Kelly. "N.A.P.'s gonna make all the other teams around here wish they'd stayed home in bed!"

For a couple of seconds everyone was quiet.

Then Gayle said, "Aren't you going to introduce us to your friend, Michael?"

"He's no friend," said Michael. "Can't you see the family resemblance?" Michael put his scrawny body at attention next to T.K.O.'s. Then he began jabbering away in his fake-o TV announcer's voice. "Presenting my cousin, Hans Pearson, eighth-grader and Coach Nilson's diving daredevil from U. City Junior High. Coach brought him over here today to try out some new moves on the board."

"I think I saw you dive," said Kelly, "at a meet this spring, against Clayton."

"Could be," Hans said, flashing his seesaw smile.

Michael cut in again. "Hans, you've just been talking to Kelly MacConnell, who did the fifty-meter butterfly this morning in thirty-eight seconds. Notice how the butterfly develops the shoulders."

"You're just jealous, Michael!" Kelly aimed her flip-flop at Michael's head and scored a hit.

But Michael didn't miss a beat. "On her right is Gayle Deckert, who swims a mean freestyle—and, upon request, a free mean-style."

Michael crossed his eyes at Gayle.

"And last, but never, *never* least," Michael continued, "is Lila Fenwick. Fenwick now holds the N.A.P. record for backstroke . . . and sunstroke."

"Funny, Michael," I told him. "Very funny."

Michael started chuckling away at his own jokes, but Hans was looking strangely—right at me.

At last he said, "You look very familiar."

"Me?" I felt my face get hot, then hotter.

"You do." Hans kept staring. "I know!" he said at last. "Jimmy Jansey! He was on Coach Nilson's team with me at U. City before he moved last year. You're his sister, aren't you?"

Jimmy Jansey's sister! I felt as if a bucket of ice water had just been thrown in my face! Jimmy Jansey's sister Jeannie was in the *third grade!* I tried to sound calm as I said, "Not me. I know her, though."

"Wow," said Hans, shaking his head in disbelief. "You look a lot like her."

I wished I were a Popsicle and could just melt away into a puddle on the hot pavement. "Maybe we're really twins," I began babbling to cover my embarrassment, "who were separated at birth by an insane nurse at the hospital."

Hans laughed. "Maybe."

"We're about to hit the snack bar," said Michael. "Adios. Ciao. Reservoir."

We watched the boys jog up the steps to the snack bar. As soon as they were out of sight, Kelly grabbed my arm and gave it a squeeze.

"Lila," she said, "he likes you."

"Really," added Gayle. "I think he just made that up about what's-his-name's sister. Just to talk to you."

I wished I could believe it, but I shook my head. "I know who he means," I said. "Jeannie Jansey. She's got glasses and long brown hair like mine. But,"

I took a breath to delay what I didn't want to hear myself say next, "Jeannie Jansey, my identical twin, just finished third grade!"

"Well," said Gayle after a second, "she's going into fourth."

"It was probably the hair," said Kelly, trying to be kind.

"Anyway," said Gayle, "he just couldn't think of anything better to say on the spur of the moment."

"Yeah," said Kelly, grinning, " 'cause he'd just fallen in *love!*"

"Get out of here!" I tried to stick my foot over Kelly's mouth, but she escaped by rolling onto Gayle's towel.

After that, while Gayle and Kelly whispered together about the muscles on Hans's body, I flipped over onto my back and pretended to close my eyes. Actually, I was squinting down at my body. I could see all the way to my toes with no problem. There wasn't the tiniest hint of a bulge anywhere until my kneecaps, if you know what I mean. Most of my friends were at least starting to get bulges in the right places. Where were mine? No wonder I'd just been mistaken for a third-grader. I must have had sunstroke to think I was looking more grown up lately. Coach was right. I was a minnow.

"Hey! Look who's here!" I heard Kelly say.

"Here she comes," sang Gayle, "Miss A-mer-i-ca!"

I raised my head and saw Rita Morgan, from our class at school, come out of the girl's locker room. I watched as she stopped and struck a pose at the top of the concrete steps. Her dark ponytail was tied with a pink scarf and she was wearing a purple bikini.

I was surprised to see Rita at the pool, since she usually hung out at the mall. "Is Rita on the swim team this year?" I asked.

Kelly and Gayle started giggling.

"Are you kidding?" Kelly whispered. "If she dove in the pool, that suit . . . "

"It would fall off!" Gayle finished for her.

We all watched then, as three guys who played football for the junior high surrounded Rita. They walked with her to the other side of the pool where the lounge chairs were. There didn't seem to be any vacant chairs, so one of the boys simply brushed someone else's towel and sunglasses off onto the pavement to make room for Rita.

We all giggled some more. But even as I giggled, I wondered what I was laughing at. Me, the Mighty Minnow, laughing at a mermaid.

The morning at the pool passed into afternoon, with more article reading, more swimming practice, and more lemonades. (My mother had strictly prohibited sodas as being "the ultimate in negative nutrition," so I was working hard to promote lemonade as the *in* drink at the pool.)

Kelly and Gayle stared at Hans so hard, they forgot to talk as he worked with Coach on his one-and-a-half-with-a-full-twist. He was a great diver, all right.

Even when he messed up and smacked the water hard with his back or stomach, he'd get back on the board and try it again. Finally he put on a T-shirt to protect his skin on the flop dives—and Gayle and Kelly kept saying they wished he'd take it off again!

As I watched, I just kept worrying about being mistaken for a third-grader. I was trying to come up with a Great Idea for what I could do about it. So far nothing had clicked.

But I kept an eye on Rita that afternoon. I watched her sashay up the steps to the snack bar, usually laughing and talking with two or three boys from the junior high. Looking hard at Rita, I realized that she was short, like me, and she didn't have all *that* much bulge to her bikini. But I bet that Rita had never been mistaken for a third-grader—probably not even when she was in the third grade! So what made the boys swarm around her like that, I wondered. After watching for a while, I decided that Rita was, as my mother would say, bursting with self-confidence. You could see it in her walk. She walked slowly, for one thing, with her head held high and her shoulders back. She looked straight ahead, not ever down. The top of her body didn't seem to move much, but with the bottom part it was a different story. A-*right* and a-*left,* and a-*right* and a-*left.* Boom, *boom,* boom, ka-*boom,* and boom, *boom,* boom, ka-*boom.*

"Lila?" Kelly held a page of her magazine in front of my face. "Let me give you this quiz on 'Your Boy Appeal.' "

"No thanks," I said. "I'd flunk."

"Come on," Gayle said. "You were the one hunko Hans talked to."

"Yeah," said Kelly. "We want to know your secrets—your Great Ideas for how to talk to boys."

Just then Rita walked right in front of our towels, talking a mile a minute to the lifeguard who had just gone on break. Boom, *boom*, boom, ka-*boom*.

I smiled to myself. A Great Idea had just strutted into my head. Even if I was built like the Mighty Minnow and even if I was wearing a navy blue tank suit and not a teeny purple bikini, I didn't have to walk like I was a measly third-grader. If short little not-too-bulgy Rita could walk like Miss America, so could I.

"I've got it," I told Kelly and Gayle. "A Great Idea for how to talk to boys."

"Spill," said Gayle.

I grinned. "You want to *talk*? Boom, *boom*! You've got to *walk*. Boom, *boom!*"

"Walk?" Kelly and Gayle looked puzzled.

"You've got to walk," I told them, "like Rita Morgan."

We turned our heads toward Rita. "See?" I counted a soft boom, *boom*, boom, ka-*boom* for them as Rita escorted the lifeguard to the snack bar. "With a sophisticated walk like that, you don't have to worry about how to talk to boys. They'll come up and start talking to you. It's all in the walk."

"Are you crazy?" said Gayle.

"I could never do that," said Kelly.

"Yes, you can!" I told them. "If I can do it, you can do it, right?"

"Lila," began Gayle, "I don't think you should. . ."

But I was already up. "I'll walk—just like Rita—to the locker room," I said, "then you do it, Kelly, and then you, Gayle. We'll watch and tell each other how we looked. Okay, here I go!" I grabbed my towel and threw it casually over my shoulder. Then, head held high and shoulders back, I began my walk. A-*left* and a-*right,* and a-*left* and a-*right.* Now *just* take your *time,* and a-*just* take your *time.*

It wasn't exactly easy, not looking down and having to count like that, but I made it to the shallow end of the pool, then turned and went past the kiddie pool. I reached the steps all right, pausing at the bottom to reconstruct in my mind an image of Rita ka-booming up. One *step* at a *time,* and one *step* at a *time,* I thought. A-*right* and a-*left,* and boom, *boom,* boom, ka-*boom.*

Confident that I was doing just fine, I took a quick look at Kelly and Gayle to see their reaction to the new me. I shouldn't have done that. They were staring at me with the oddest expressions on their faces. It must have been those expressions, their eyes wide open and their mouths a little bit open, too, that made me *ka* where I should have *boomed.* My foot slipped. I put my hands out to stop my fall, but not before both knees hit hard on the concrete step below me and then scraped down to the step under that.

I lay face down on the steps, feeling a funny numbness in my knees. I wondered if I could move. Maybe I was paralyzed. I heard bare feet running up the steps behind me.

"Lila! Are you okay?" Gayle knelt down beside me. Gripping her hand, I turned over and sat up slowly, afraid I'd cry if I tried to talk.

"Boy! Your knees are really bleeding!" said Kelly. "I'll get some wet paper towels." She raced into the locker room.

"Gayle," I said in a croaky whisper, "you think . . . everybody . . . that T.K.O. . . . . saw me take this spill?"

"Don't worry," Gayle said. "I think Kelly and I were the only ones watching." She handed me my glasses, which had skidded across the pavement. "Listen, Lila, your knees look pretty bad. Coach should look at them. Will you be okay by yourself for a second while I go get him?"

I nodded, scooching myself over to the side of the steps by the concrete wall and hoping that I looked invisible. I bit the insides of my cheeks to keep the tears from coming.

I shoved on my specs and saw, to my surprise, that three kiddie pool kids had climbed halfway up the steps. They were staring silently at my knees.

One little boy, his bright green-and-yellow swim ring still around his middle, pointed a stubby finger at my knees.

"Big boo-boos," he said.

"Yes," I managed to groan, "but I'm okay. You can all go back to the pool now. Go on."

None of them moved.

"Big boo-boo," the little boy said, pointing to a scab on his own fat knee. Then, as he looked at his knee, he opened his mouth and began wailing at the top of his lungs. "Boo-boo!" he cried. "Booooooooo-booooooo!"

"Shhhh! Quiet!" I told him. "Your boo-boo is all better now!" But it was too late. People began rushing from all directions to see why he was howling. A woman in a zebra print bathing suit scooped up the shrieking toddler and carried him off. I searched for Kelly or Gayle in the faces that were fast gathering around me but found Michael instead. His usually grinning face looked worried. Next to him was T.K.O. He looked worried, too, and I noticed that, like his smile, his frown was sort of lopsided.

"Oh, gross!" Rita Morgan burst through to the center of the crowd. "I can see all the way to her *bone!*" She knelt beside me and put her hand on my forehead, as if she thought I had a fever. "Lila, you poor thing!" she cooed loudly. "Your knees are going to be scarred for life!"

"Move it!" Kelly squeezed between Rita and me and covered my knees with wet paper towels.

As if out of nowhere, Coach Nilson's face appeared, close to mine. He peeled back the paper towels. The bleeding had gone from a flood to a steady drizzle. "Boy, I bet that hurts," he said.

The tears began spilling onto my cheeks now.

Kelly handed me a new paper towel while Coach went on, "You may even need a couple stitches."

"Stitches!" I was suddenly dry-eyed. "Hey, it's just skinned knees!"

"Well," said Coach, "we'll see. First I want to use plenty of soap and water on them." Coach looked around for a minute. "Michael! Hans!" he called. "Can you guys come over here and give Lila a hand?"

"Coach! No!" I nearly shouted. "I don't need a hand!"

"You don't need a hand," said Michael, squatting down next to me. "You need new knees."

"Help Lila over to my station, will you, fellows?" Coach said. Then he stood up and waved his arms at the kids gathered around me on the steps. "Everyone else, clear out. I don't want to see the rest of you anywhere near my station." Coach turned back to me and said, "I'm going to get a container of hot water."

I put one arm around Michael's scrawny neck. I hesitated a moment, with my other arm hovering over Hans's neck. Then, what could I do? I put my arm around his shoulders. I was surprised at how warm his skin was. I felt my face turning as red as my knees!

The three of us hobbled over to Coach's umbrella table, where he kept his first aid kit, with Kelly and Gayle not far behind. When Coach came back, he pressed my knees with two clean cloths to stop the bleeding. Then, with hot water and soap, he gently washed them and put on some ointment. He put an enormous square gauze pad over one knee and stuck it on with adhesive tape.

"Fenwick," said Michael after the first knee was bandaged, "you look like a movie star!"

"I know, Michael," I said, "from *The Mummy's Revenge*, right?"

"Don't steal my punch lines, Fenwick," Michael growled, "less'n you want your kneecaps broke."

"You're too late for that," Hans told him. "You'll have to break her elbows."

"Hey, cool it!" said Gayle.

"Right," Coach said. "Lila needs medical attention, not a comedy routine." He finished putting what he called a butterfly bandage on my other knee and covered it with another big gauze pad. "I don't think you'll need any stitches, but it looks like N.A.P. will have to find a replacement backstroker for Saturday."

"You'll never replace me, Coach." I managed a small smile.

"You're right," he said. "We might as well call off the meet." He gave me a fast rub on the head. "By the way, Lila, how'd you get to practice this morning?"

"On my bike," I told him.

"Guess you'll need a ride home," he said.

"Guess so. I'll call my mom."

"You live just off Clayton Road, don't you?" asked Coach.

I nodded.

Coach looked at his watch. "I can drop you off. I'm driving the wagon and there's plenty of room for your bike in the back." He turned to Gayle and Kelly. "Can you girls get Lila's things?"

As Gayle and Kelly sprinted toward the locker room, Coach checked my bandages again. "Think you can walk?" he asked.

I stood up and took a few painful steps. Michael put an arm around me and together we made our way to the parking lot. Gayle met us by Coach's car, a big turquoise-and-white 1950's station wagon. She tossed my pack in through a window. Kelly wheeled my bike over and helped Coach lift it into the back.

"Front passenger door's jammed," Coach told me. "You'll have more room in the back anyway, Lila."

Slowly and stiffly, with as little knee bending as possible, I got into the backseat.

"I'll call you later," said Gayle.

Then, to my surprise, Hans got into the backseat beside me. He must have noticed the puzzled look on my face, because he said, "Coach is my ride home too." He slammed the door.

As Coach started up his engine, I gave Michael a little wave. He was standing off to one side of the parking lot, looking like a sad stray dog.

Then I looked over at Gayle and Kelly, and for a

second I thought they had both lost their minds. There they were, grinning away and jumping up and down like some kind of lunatic cheerleaders. Gayle waved like mad and Kelly held up two crossed fingers, as if wishing me luck. Then it hit me. *They think I'm lucky! Even though my knees are in critical condition, they think I'm lucky because I get to ride home with T.K.O.!*

That's when it came to me, the magazine article *I* could write called "How to Talk to Boys." I could give Great Advice! And it wouldn't be to ask the score of some baseball game to show you were interested in sports either.

"Talking to boys isn't hard," I'd begin, "but it can be painful. For starters, just look three years younger than your real age so a boy will mistake you for a friend's little sister. Next, skin your knees. That way you can always talk about boo-boos."

My mind was so occupied with my article that when Hans spoke, I barely heard him.

"Oh, sorry," I said. "What did you say?"

"I was just wondering," said Hans, "about the Cardinals game today against the Mets. Did you happen to hear the score?"

HOW TO MAKE THE BEST OF IT

That's what my mom said to me. She said, "Well, Lila, you'll just have to make the best of it." Maybe you think she was referring to my super-skinned-up knees and how I'd be sitting out at swimming practice for a while, but that wasn't the reason. She said, "Make the best of it" after my dad told me *his* Great Idea for our summer vacation.

The bad news hit last night at dinner. We were eating cabbage-smothered chicken, which in itself was pretty bad news. The cabbage was deep purple, and it stained the chicken a dark blue-black color. It was hard to look at and even harder to swallow, but my mom had read that vegetables in the cabbage family were full of fiber, and she believed in fiber, so we had cabbage-smothered chicken about once a week. If only Gayle could eat dinner at our house, I thought, she wouldn't have to worry about going away to a fat camp.

My dad had pushed his chair back from the table and looked at his watch. One of his patients had just phoned to say her contractions were three minutes apart. My dad would have to go to the hospital to meet her before long. He's an obstetrician, a doctor who helps women have their babies. He didn't deliver me though. He says doctors can't operate on people in their own families. He claims that's why he won't pierce my ears.

"How are the knees today?" he asked me.

"Much better," I told him, poking a glob of cabbage under my chicken bones to hide it. "You think I could get these gonzo pads off and switch to Band-Aids?"

"Maybe tomorrow," said my dad. "What does Coach say about your swimming?"

"He says I'm out for at least another week, if not more."

"Then a little vacation wouldn't interrupt your swimming career, would it?"

"I guess not," I told him. "Why?"

My dad peered over his glasses at my mom. "You haven't told Lila, Fran?"

"I haven't had a chance even to think about these

plans of yours, Phil. I had an exam this afternoon." My mom had just gone back to college for a degree in physical education. She wanted to teach—not at the junior high or anything like that, thank goodness—but older women, around her age, who needed help with exercise and nutrition.

My dad leaned back in his chair. "This morning Shannon asked us if we'd mind swapping vacation times with her," my dad said.

Shannon is my father's partner in the baby business. *Us* is my father. This is the way he always talks about himself. I finally figured out that it's because he has a twin brother and growing up there'd always been the two of them. But now, even when his brother isn't right there beside him, he's still *we* and *us*.

"So," my dad was saying, "we can leave on Sunday."

"For where?" I wanted to know.

"For Ironvale!" he told me grandly. "We're going to spend two weeks at Camp Ironvale!"

"Camp Ironvale?" I'd heard that name before but couldn't think when. It wasn't one of the campgrounds we'd been to before. "Where is it?"

"It's about an hour and a half from here. Near Ironton in the Ozarks. We'll be acting M.D. for two weeks, so it won't be a total vacation for us, but a few cases of poison ivy and sunburn will certainly be a change from what we're used to. And no night calls!"

"I don't get it." I looked at my dad grinning away. "If it's a vacation, why are you working? And what's all this about poison ivy?"

"What don't you understand, honey?" my dad asked. "We're going to spend two weeks at Ironvale. We'll be the camp doctor and have office hours each morning, but you and your mother will be free to do whatever you want—off schedule, that is. There's a great big swimming dock at the lake, horses, an archery range, lots of nature trails—perfect for your birding, Fran—and there's Eagle Peak. Have we ever told you the legend of Eagle Peak? It is said that anyone who spends the night there, out in the open, under the stars—"

"Wait! Hold it!" I interrupted. "What kind of camp is this? Parents go with their kids?"

"No, no. Parents don't go with the campers," my dad said. "You won't be a regular camper. You'll be what's called a 'stray.' There may be a few other strays, usually are, but most of the campers will be Scouts, Lila. Ironvale is a Boy Scout camp."

I stared at my father, then shook my head a little to clear it. "*Boy* Scout camp? We're going to a Boy Scout camp? Are you serious?"

"Serious as a sinusitis," said my dad.

"What's sinusitis?"

"A runny nose."

"Dad! I can't believe this!" I said. "What a weird idea for a vacation! I'm supposed to go to Boy Scout camp?" I turned to my mom. "You want to go?"

"Can't wait!" she said.

"But I'll be the only girl around hundreds of boys—like some sort of freak!" I groaned to my father. "How would you like it?"

"I do find myself the only man around plenty of women every day—women having babies!" My dad smiled.

"I haven't been to Ironvale for years," said my mom, reaching over with her fork and lifting up my chicken bones to reveal my stash of cabbage. "But your father and I used to go nearly every summer before you were born. We'd stay at the Health Lodge with Grace and Big Joe Lindquist." A look of sadness crossed my mom's face and she turned to my dad. "It won't be the same without Big Joe, will it?" she said.

I'd never met the Lindquists. They lived in Kansas City. But I'd heard stories about them from my mom and dad. And I knew how upset my parents had been this spring when they got the news that Big Joe had died of a heart attack.

My dad shook his head. "No, it won't be the same, that's for sure."

My mom sighed and then looked back at me. "Ironvale is a beautiful place, honey. You'll love it. Wait and see. As I remember, there were always plenty of strays. The camp director's children aren't always all boys, and the kids of the people who run the kitchen sometimes come to camp. There'll be a real gang of kids, all different ages, who do things together."

"We'll bet you dollars to doughnuts that at the end of two weeks, you won't want to come home!" said my dad. "Anyway, Grace Lindquist is camp nurse and her three children are there with her—twin boys and a girl. Andrew and Joey should be about seven or eight by now and Kari—let's see—Kari must be about ready for high school."

"Oh, great!" I said. "I bet a high school girl is going to just love hanging around with an almost-sixth-grader." Besides, I thought, she'll probably think I'm her brothers' age.

I groaned again, and that's when my mom gave me her Great Advice. "Well, Lila," she said, "you'll just have to make the best of it."

My mom is always giving me Great Advice like that. *Make the best of it* or *Wait and see* or *Look at the bright side.* I try to tune out, but it's not that easy. When you hear these things often enough, they seep into your brain.

Make the best of it. Make the best of it. Well, if I just didn't have to be the only girl my age, then it might be okay.

"Maybe if I took a friend . . . " I began. "Or two."

"Fine with me," said my mom.

My dad nodded. "Sure."

Gayle and Kelly would jump at the chance to come with us! I envisioned their faces, beaming with gratitude as I offered them this opportunity to spend two weeks among hundreds and hundreds of boys. Now I was seeing things a little differently. I could hardly wait to invite them.

"This could be great!" I said.

"We're happy you think so," said my dad, checking his watch. "We'd better run if we want to beat that baby to the hospital." He took his plate into the kitchen and then headed for the garage.

"Think you'll be home late, Phil?" my mom called to him.

"Shouldn't be," he called back. "It's this mother's third."

As the garage door went up, I said to my mom, "I still can't believe we're going to a Boy Scout camp! It's so . . . strange!"

"You know your father, Lila." My mom looked amused.

"What is there to do at Ironvale?" I asked her.

"Well, I know that it's a great place for birding," she began.

"Thrilling!" I told her. When I was in second grade, my mom had given me this little green leather book so that I could keep a list, the way she did, of all the birds I saw. I spent one afternoon looking out the window at the backyard bird feeder and I saw a cardinal, a blue jay, a chickadee, and a sparrow. That was as far as I'd gotten: four birds in four years.

"Let's see," she went on, "you can swim off the

dock in Lake Coleman and in dozens of gorgeous crystal-clear streams."

"But I can't swim until my knees get better. This is not sounding too terrific, Mom!"

"There's Eagle Peak," my mom added.

"Oh, right. Dad started saying something about some legend?"

My mom nodded. "It is said," she began, using the same words my father had used, "that if you climb to the top of Eagle Peak and spend the night there, under the stars, you will discover something— some particular thing about yourself that you've never known before."

"Eagle Peak," I said. "But it's only a legend, right?"

My mom just smiled mysteriously.

"What else?" I asked her.

"There's horseback riding!" My mom laughed. "This could be your big opportunity to learn to ride a horse, Lila—right side up!"

"Oh, sure," I said, not wanting to remember the time when I was five and had gone on a pony ride. Somehow or other the belt that held the saddle on the pony had worked itself loose and every time the pony took a step, I tilted farther and farther to the side until suddenly I was hanging upside down under that pony, clutching the saddle for all I was worth. Ever since then, horseback riding has been the number one item on my list of "Things I Never Want to Do Again."

"Now I've got a deal you can't refuse," my mom

said, getting up from the table. "I'll take your turn doing dishes if you'll help me go over my first aid while I work."

"You're on," I said. Since my ka-boom disaster, I had taken a new interest in quizzing my mom for her first aid exam. I'd already found out that Coach used butterfly bandages to hold flaps of my skin together so that I wouldn't need stitches. I was grateful that he'd passed his first aid exam!

I got her book, *First Aid Procedures*, and sat on a stool beside the counter while she began rinsing the dishes. I flipped to the review section.

"Okay," I began, "I happen to have experience with this first question, so I'll know if you flub it: What's the first aid for heavy bleeding?"

"Press gauze or a clean cloth directly over the wound," my mom recited.

"Then what should you check for?"

"Shock," said my mom.

"And the symptoms of shock are . . . "

"Pale, cold, clammy skin, mottled in color. Breathing is weak and shallow or it may be deep but irregular. The victim is apathetic . . . "

"Apa . . . what?"

"Apathetic. Doesn't care what's going on around him."

I thought back to last week, to the steps of N.A.P. "I wish I'd been in shock when I skinned my knees," I told my mom. "Then I wouldn't have cared about everybody staring at me."

"Lila! Don't wish that! Shock is serious. It has to be treated quickly. If it isn't, a person's blood pressure can drop so low that the heart will stop pumping." My mom looked at me. "People die from shock," she said.

"I take it back! I take it back!" I told her, looking again at the book. "What is the first aid procedure for shock?"

"Place a blanket over the victim if he is cold or damp. Elevate the legs eight to twelve inches. This helps send blood back toward the heart and keeps it beating. Check for breathing and for heartbeat by looking for a pulse in the neck."

We went on like this until my mom had told me the correct treatment for everything from blisters to snake bites.

"You'll ace the exam, Mom," I said. "No sweat."

"I hope you're right, Lila," she said, reaching down, without bending her knees at all, to pick up a sliver of cabbage that had dropped on the floor. You'd think all her sessions on the Body Toner Rowing Machine would be enough for her, but no. My mom would use any excuse—like picking up a piece of cabbage—to exercise. She'd even bought herself a set of weights and was starting to pump iron! It seemed pretty strange to have a mother with hair that was turning gray—salt and pepper was how she put it—who dressed in sweat suits like all her jock friends from the college. But even with her hair she looked a lot younger than most of my friends' moms. Maybe I got my Jeannie-Jansey-third-grade looks from her, I thought.

"Thanks for the help, Lila," my mom said. "Now I've got to go upstairs and study my class notes."

"Any time," I told her. "Any time."

I sat on the kitchen stool, spinning it back and forth for a while, thinking and planning just how I'd tell Gayle and Kelly about Boy Scout camp. I had a good thing to offer and I wanted to make the best of it.

The next morning I sat on my towel in the shade at N.A.P. and watched my friends swim laps. It was boring, but in a way I didn't mind because I loved imagining what Gayle and Kelly would do when I asked them to come to Ironvale. Gayle would hug me and then ham it up, I thought, go into some crazy routine, but I pictured Kelly simply saying over and over, "Oh, thank you, Lila! Thank you!"

After morning practice Kelly and Gayle came and sat down with me. Across the grass on the far side of the pool, I saw Michael Watson doing pushups. If he had a ray of hope that he could build up his skinny body, I should be hopeful about mine, I thought. He must have felt me watching him, because he looked up at me and then came sprinting over.

He did a strange sort of salute. "Well, Fenwick,"

he said, "are you really ready to be trustworthy, loyal, helpful, friendly, courteous, kind, obedient, cheerful—"

"What are you talking about, weirdo?" I asked him.

"You know, Fenwick," he said. "Those are the Boy Scout Laws!"

I grinned at Michael. The news had certainly gotten out quickly. Now all I had to do was sit here and make the best of it.

"How'd you find out where I'm going?" I asked him.

"My mom ran into your dad at the drugstore this morning," said Michael. "She said he's taking you all to Ironvale and he's really excited about it."

"What's Ironvale?" Kelly asked.

"I didn't know you were going away," said Gayle. "Why didn't you tell us?"

"I just found out last night," I told them. "My dad is going to be the doctor at this Boy Scout camp for a couple of weeks and I'm going to go too."

"Lila!" Kelly shrieked. "That's so great!"

"Yeah," I admitted. "I guess it is."

By the end of the lunch break most of the girls on the N.A.P. team were sitting around my towel listening to me tell about hiking and swimming and the legend of Eagle Peak at Boy Scout camp. And even though I was barefoot, I had every single one of them wishing that she were in my shoes.

Just before the start of afternoon practice, I called Gayle and Kelly into a huddle.

"Listen," I whispered, "I didn't want to say this in front of everybody, but my parents said I could ask you guys to come with us to Ironvale—to Boy Scout camp!"

I stood there, waiting for the hugs and the tears of gratitude, but all I got were frozen stares.

"What's the matter?" I asked, looking from Gayle to Kelly. "Don't you want to go?"

"Want to?" said Gayle. "I'd give up chocolate chip cookies for a month if I could go! But my mom's already sent in the check for Echo Hills. I'm signed, sealed, and delivered to fat camp!"

"Oh, come on!" I told her. "What if you got appendicitis? Or broke a leg? They'd have to let you out of it and give you your money back."

"Only a fifty percent refund," she told me. "I read the contract."

I turned to Kelly. "What about you?" I asked.

"Lila," Kelly said, "can you imagine what Coach would do if I took off for two weeks? You're already out because of your knees, but if I left . . . "

She didn't even have to finish. I knew she was right. Coach would flip if Kelly said she was leaving. She was his best all-around swimmer, just about the only one who could keep N.A.P. from sinking into a deep sleep.

"I wish I could!" Kelly said. "Maybe you can think of something. . . . "

But as the whistle blew for the beginning of afternoon practice, I knew that I couldn't pull a sneaky

Great Idea for getting Kelly off the team. Not on Coach.

I lay on my towel for a long time, imagining myself a lonely stray, with my father, Chief Poison Ivy Checker, and my mother, whose idea of a good time was hanging around in the woods gawking at birds. Just as I was beginning to imagine becoming desperate enough to try horseback riding, a pair of feet stepped onto my towel. Feet with toenails painted pink. The feet of Rita Morgan.

Rita sat down beside me. "How are your knees, Lila?" she asked, not really looking at me but checking out the starting blocks where six boys were on their marks. "You really did a number on them. I swear, I think I could see your bone!"

"They're okay," I told her.

"Oh, by the way," Rita said, riveting her gaze directly on me now. "I heard you were going to *Boy* Scout camp."

Maybe it was because my ka-booms had been such an utter flop, but suddenly I wanted—*really* wanted—to make Rita Morgan turn green with envy over my summer vacation.

"Yeah," I said. "We're leaving on Sunday."

"Oooh, Lila," breathed Rita. "You are sooooo lucky!"

"I guess Boy Scout camp will be a lot different from N.A.P.," I said. "I mean, for one thing, there'll be boys everywhere. I guess there'll be so many boys around that it'll be practically impossible to get away from them."

"You get to eat with them and stuff?" she asked.

"Oh, sure," I told her. "And after dinner, when it's all dark, you walk down these trails to a big campfire and sit under the stars, close together, in a big circle."

Rita's ever-huge blue eyes looked as if they were headed for a new world's record in the wide-open category. I kept going.

"And you know, the Scouts at this camp aren't just peewee Cub Scouts."

"No?"

"No, they're older—mostly in junior high and high school, I think. About the same age as that lifeguard." I nodded toward the lifeguard's stand and then looked back at Rita. That's when I noticed her skin—just after I'd said the word *lifeguard.* Her legs, her arms, the space between the top and bottom of her bikini looked faintly green.

Wow! I thought. Am I actually doing it? Am I making Rita turn green with envy? I blinked my eyes and then opened them again to make sure I wasn't seeing things. But she was green all right—just a faint tint, the color of lime Jell-O.

"And there's this place," I went on, "Eagle Peak, and if you camp out there, under the stars, it's supposed to be sort of magical and you find out something that you never knew before. About yourself."

If Rita camped out there, would she discover that she had the ability to turn green? Would she stay this color forever? Could she feel it? She hadn't seemed to notice yet. I wondered if she would get greener and greener the more I talked. Then I wondered if I could make Rita fade to her basic pink again. I thought I'd try and see.

"Well," I said, thinking fast, "there are lots of boys, but there are also lots of snakes. My dad said that sometimes they swarm around on the trails and it's hard not to step on them."

"Oh, gross! Don't even say that!" Rita looked like she might lose whatever it was she'd just had at the snack bar. But she didn't lose her green tinge.

"And I think you have to use a latrine."

"A what?"

"An outside toilet. It's just a board with a hole cut out of it over—"

"I get the picture," said the still-green Rita.

I was starting to get worried about her color. It didn't look at all healthy.

Rita looked at her toes then and held her fingertips down next to them, as if checking to see whether her polish all matched.

I looked down past my bandaged knees to my toes. They were plain ugly skinny little toes. My toenails were ragged or had been torn off in a hurry, leaving only a tiny strip of nail.

It must have been seeing Rita's feet, those ten pretty

pearl pink piggies, that wiggled such a strange Great Idea into my head.

Ask Rita to go to Boy Scout camp, came the message from my brain.

Rita? I couldn't believe I'd heard it right. *Ask Rita?*

Do it! urged the voice inside my skull. *She's just the one to teach you how to be sophisticated.*

But look how my ka-boom imitation turned out, I protested.

Okay, so that was a bit of a mess. My brain was whirling now. *But if you spent more time with Rita—a genuine two-week crash course—she could teach you what you need to know to look and act older!*

That did sound tempting!

But wait! Spending two weeks with Rita would drive me crazy! I argued.

True, agreed my brain, *but what's a little craziness when you could learn so much! Look at her toes! Go ahead, look at them. They're perfect. Then look at what you call toes. Blechh! You need help growing up! The sooner the better! S.O.S!*

A little thrill ran through me. *You really think she could? Help me change from the Mighty Minnow to a Mermaid?*

Absolutely! said my brain. *Do it!*

Rita was still examining her nails. And her skin still matched the grass. I was getting nervous. Maybe if Rita knew she could come with me, she'd stop turning green.

"Listen, Rita," I began, "my parents said it was okay if I asked a friend to go to camp with us."

Rita just stared at me.

"So, you think maybe you'd like to come?" I asked.

"Me?" Rita asked. "Lila, are you serious?"

"Sure," I said.

"Ohhh, Lila!" Rita squealed. "I'd love to! I'd really love to! I'm sure it'll be okay with Mother and Daddy. Oh, gosh! I can't believe it!"

Just then Coach's whistle blew again, signaling the end of afternoon practice. As kids lifted themselves out of the pool and headed for the snack bar, Rita looked at her watch. "Oh, my gosh!" she cried. "I was only supposed to leave this stuff on for ten minutes!" She sprang up from my towel.

"What stuff?" I asked.

"This!" Rita tossed a little white tube in my direction. "Try it," she said to me over her shoulder. "You could use some. I'll call you tonight, okay? I'm so excited! See you, Lila!"

I examined the tube in my hand. Miracle Tanning Gel, the label said. Get a fabulous two-hour tan in ten minutes! I unscrewed the lid and squeezed a little bit of the gel onto my finger—a little glob of lime green.

I watched Rita doing a fast ka-boom toward the girls' locker room until she was lost in the mob of kids swarming up the steps. Was asking Rita to come to Ironvale with me a Great Idea, I wondered? Or could this turn out to be the very Worst Idea I'd ever had?

I'll just have to wait and see, I thought. I'll look at the bright side. And some way or other, I'll make the best of it.

HOW TO
DRIVE YOUR
PARENTS CRAZY

"I can't believe it! I can't believe it!" Gayle kept saying when I called that night to tell her that I'd asked Rita to come with me to Boy Scout camp.

"Listen, Gayle," I said, "I need help seeming my age. And Rita's sort of my size and all, but she looks—and acts—much older. She's sophisticated! So one reason I asked her to go is to get some tips from her on how never to be mistaken for a third grader again!" I paused. "You've got fat camp, I've got Rita."

"That's *one* reason you're taking Rita," my math whiz friend said. "You have a second reason?"

"It's my father," I said. "He goes around the house singing camp songs and he's so gung ho about this trip, it's driving me crazy! Can you think of a better way to get even with him than to make him put up with Rita for two weeks?"

Gayle had to laugh. "Lila," she said, "your mind is frightening!"

"I know," I said. "It's the perfect way to drive him crazy!"

"But," Gayle pointed out, "she'll drive you crazy too."

"Probably," I admitted. "This is not the most perfect Great Idea I've ever had, but still, it'll be worth it if I can learn the S.O.S."

"The *what?*"

"S.O.S.," I told Gayle. "Secrets of Sophistication."

At dawn on leaving-for-camp Sunday, my dad marched into my room, singing, *"It's time to get up, it's time to get up, it's time to get up in the morning!"*

I opened one eye enough to discover that he was wearing a brown shirt with a red something under the chin. I opened the other eye and saw that he had on brown shorts and knee socks.

"I'm having a bad dream," I muttered to myself, pulling the covers over my head.

"Rise and shine, Lila!" My dad yanked the quilt off my bed. "It's a beautiful day for going to Camp Ironvale!"

"I'm up. I'm up." I swiveled into a sitting position on the edge of my bed. When I put on my specs, I saw that the red blur was a bandana around my dad's neck. It was held in place by a giant hollowed-out lobster claw, bright orange. I wondered if other fathers ever dressed like this. Then I wondered why I'd ever thought it was a Great Idea to have Rita drive my father crazy—he was crazy enough already!

My dad picked up the duffel bag I'd packed the night before. He looked inside and smiled. "Nice work, Lila! Is everything you'll need in here?"

"Every single thing," I told him.

My dad slung the bag over his shoulder. "Good! We'll be able to add our things to this bag with no problem." He marched out of my room, chanting, "It's always right to pack 'em light! A heavy pack can break your back!"

I rolled my eyes up to the ceiling.

If I've heard this philosophy once, I've heard it a hundred times. My father is the number one expert packer of the world. Before he packs a suitcase or a duffel bag, he lays all his clothes out on his bed to make sure he doesn't forget anything. He packs the flat things first, and then he rolls his underpants and undershirts into little sausages and wedges them into any leftover spaces.

I could hear him whistling now as he arranged our duffel bag with what he'd need for two weeks at Ironvale.

I brushed my hair and teeth and splashed some water on my face, then pulled on a St. Louis Zoo T-shirt with a chimpanzee on the front and a pair of navy blue shorts. I put on my sneakers without socks and peeked at my knees under the Band-Aids. They didn't look at all like raw meat any more. As I thumped, stiff legged, down to breakfast, I hoped I could go swimming sooner than I'd thought.

My mom was eating a bowl of cereal. "Morning, honey. Can I pour you some?"

"Is it that cardboard stuff you like?" I peered into her bowl. "No thanks. I'll have some Cheerios."

My dad came down, still whistling, duffel bag in hand. He took two eggs from a carton in the fridge.

"The moment of truth is almost at hand," he said, cracking each egg one-handed into a cast-iron skillet. "Now we'll see if the trunk space in our new Buick is all that the salesman claimed it was."

"It certainly looks enormous," said my mom, giving my dad a funny smile. "In fact, it looked so big that I didn't think you'd mind if I put something in already."

"You put something in? What?" My dad looked almost hurt. Packing was his job.

"My weights," my mom explained. "I didn't want two weeks of camp to put me behind with my training."

"Those two-ton dumbbells of yours are in our new trunk!?"

"Not dumbbells," my mom said. "Weights."

"Fran, don't you think it might be too much for the car? It's brand-new! We don't want to overdo it on the first trip."

"If I can lift the weights," said my mom, "the car can handle them."

My dad muttered something under his breath. Then he turned to me. "Think you should give Rita a call?" he asked. "Make sure she's up and at 'em?"

"I told her we'd be there at eight on the dot," I said. "She'll be ready."

I started to say that Rita was so anxious to check out the Boy Scouts, she'd be waiting on the curb, but I didn't want to start explaining Rita to my parents. They'd heard a little bit about her over the years we'd been together in school—how we all thought she was such a prissy flirt and called her Miss Perfect—so they'd been surprised when I told them that the friend I'd invited on our trip was Rita. But what they didn't know was that the very same boys who used to yell "Cooties!" and run away when Rita came near them were now practically tripping over their own feet to be near her. They also didn't know that Rita was going to be my S.O.S. teacher this summer. And Rita didn't know it either.

We all did a few last-minute chores then. My dad called to have the paper stopped and went out to work on his masterpiece of a trunk-packing job. My mom wrapped up some fruit for us to eat in the car. I stuck a "vacation feeder" into the gravel on the bottom of my guppy tank and told my fish goodbye.

When we pulled up to Rita's house, she wasn't on the curb, but her father was out on the front lawn. He was up and at 'em, all right, dressed in a suit with a vest and pulling crabgrass blades from what looked to me like a perfect, golf course lawn. I wondered what he would think of my father, dressed in his oversize Boy Scout uniform, but he didn't even seem to notice.

Mr. Morgan shook hands with my mom and dad. He took a walk all around our new Buick and then started telling my parents all about their latest car and its computerized systems. He pointed to the driveway where it sat, silver and sparkling clean. The seats inside were bright red and a bumper sticker on the back read "Born to shop."

I walked up the sidewalk to get Rita. Just as I reached out for the heavy golden door knocker, Mrs. Morgan opened the front door. She was wearing a lacy lavender robe, and her yellow hair was piled on top of her head, every strand in place.

"Hi, Mrs. Morgan," I said. "Is Rita ready?"

Before Mrs. Morgan had a chance to answer, my mother jogged up behind me to talk to her. My mom was wearing her gray sweat suit and sneakers. I wished that Rita's mother could give my mom a few lessons in S.O.S.

"We're so glad that Rita is going with us to Ironvale," my mom said. "Here's the camp address and phone number." She handed Rita's mother a folded note.

Mrs. Morgan slipped it absently into the pocket of her robe. "I just can't imagine why Rita wants to go camping," she said. "It's not her style—not at all."

She looked at us vacantly for a moment, as if she'd forgotten why we were standing on her front porch. "Well, I'll see if she's ready."

She turned her head away from us and gave a shrill yodel, "Riiiiiita!"

"Five seconds!" came Rita's voice from inside the house.

Mrs. Morgan didn't invite us in or anything. I guessed that she didn't want us tromping on the fluffy white carpet that she was standing on in her delicate, purple, high-heeled slippers—slippers with aqua feathers on the toes.

At last I caught sight of Rita coming down the hallway. She seemed to be dragging something. Her mother turned away from us to talk to her daughter.

"Remember what I told you now," her mother said, "about the eating."

"Okay, Mother," said Rita.

"You gain weight at that camp and you're going on Scarsdale for the rest of the summer, and I mean it."

"Okay!" Rita said. "Okay!"

Mrs. Morgan faced us again. "Camps serve too much peanut butter," she complained. "Peanut butter goes straight to her thighs!" She gave the top of Rita's leg a little smack. "If she doesn't watch it, she'll have cellulite before her sixteenth birthday."

"Get off my back, Mom," Rita said in a low voice that I didn't think we were supposed to hear.

Then Rita stepped around the purple figure of her mother and flashed us a smile. She looked up and

at 'em, too, in hot pink short shorts and a pink hal-
ter top with white ruffles around the armholes. Her
ponytail was perched even higher than usual on the
back of her head, and she was holding onto the handle of an enormous powder blue Samsonite suitcase.
My whole family had packed in two medium-sized
duffel bags!

"Want some help with that?" I asked. The two of
us managed to guide the suitcase, which had four
little-bitty wheels on the bottom, to our car.

"Bye, Daddy!" Rita blew her father a kiss.

"Bye, princess!" her father said. "Don't you give
these people any trouble, you hear?" He turned to
my father, "If she's any trouble, just send her back
home."

"The girls will be fine," my dad said. "Ironvale
brings out the best in everyone." As he spoke, he
was eyeing Rita's suitcase. "Morning, Rita," he said.
"Say, that's a monster of a suitcase. Is everything in
there necessary?"

Rita nodded. "Every single thing," she assured him.
"I've just got one more little load to bring out." Rita
breezed back into her house and returned rolling a
slightly smaller matching suitcase.

I had to smile when I saw my father's face—Rita
was driving him crazy all ready! He stood beside the
trunk of our new car, looking at Rita's suitcases and
scratching his head. Then he clapped his hands together, as if cheering himself on, and said, "Well!"

My dad started taking our things out of the trunk.

When everything was on the curb, he put Rita's largest suitcase on the bottom of the trunk and her other suitcase on top of that. Then he began to fit my mom's weights, our duffel bags, backpacks, knapsacks, and other smaller items around them. Pretty soon the trunk looked like a mountainous jigsaw puzzle, with a cooler shape here and a hiking boot shape there.

"Nice work," I told him when the last piece was in place.

"Now if we can just close the lid," he said. He tried half a dozen times without success. Then my muscle mom came to the rescue, but even the two of them couldn't slam that trunk shut.

Out onto the curb came the duffel bags, the cooler, the hiking boots. Out came the backpacks, the fishing rods, the life jackets. Out came my mother's weights and, at last, out came the Samsonite twins.

On the second try, by leaving out one of the Samsonites, my dad managed to do it. But by the time he shut the trunk, I noticed he had big circles of sweat under the arms of his Boy Scout shirt.

"Okay," he called, a little less cheerfully than before. "All aboard for Ironvale!"

My mom slid in behind the wheel of the car and my dad sat beside her. Rita and I wedged ourselves into the backseat on either side of Rita's suitcase. We all buckled up.

"This car seems really smooth," Rita announced. "I probably won't even feel carsick at all."

My mom turned around and looked at Rita with concern. "Are you prone to car sickness, honey?"

"I *do* have a delicate stomach," Rita said. "But like I said, this car will probably be really smooth."

"Just let me know in time if you want me to pull over," said my mom, giving my dad a quick look. "Off we go!"

I hadn't prepared my parents for Rita, but already—just five minutes into the trip—they were getting a pretty good idea of what was in store for them during the next two weeks. But now, sitting in the car, I realized that I hadn't prepared Rita for the way my parents acted either. Not at all! Their idea for starting a trip off right is to sing.

> *"The ants go marching one by one, hurrah! Hurrah!"*
> they began singing,
> *"The ants go marching one by one, hurrah! Hurrah!"*

Rita looked at me in amazement. I just shrugged and spiraled my finger around my ear, making a little cuckoo sign.

> *"The ants go marching one by one*
> *The little one stops to shoot the gun*
> *And they all go marching. . ."*

I wished I could tell Rita that these weren't my real parents—that I'd been left on their doorstep in a basket. I thought about repeating what I'd said that day at the pool, to T.K.O. Hans, about an insane nurse at the hospital switching babies, but before I could think how to put it, my dad stopped singing the ant song and started talking to my mom about the old days.

"You know, we've never been to Ironvale without Big Joe," he began. "I remember once we went on an overnight to Eagle Peak and he thought we'd packed the tent and we thought he'd packed it. . . . "

"So what's in your suitcases?" I whispered to Rita, hoping to divert her from my dad's scouting story. He was still driving me nuts!

"In the big one, clothes, mostly," she told me. "I didn't know exactly what to bring, so I just brought everything. Know what I mean?"

"Sort of," I said.

"And look in here," Rita said, pushing the little silver catches on her Samsonite to open it. She lifted the lid and revealed a jumble of bottles, jars, tubes, a gleaming violet hair dryer, and an enormous plastic bag labeled Beauty Puffs. If my father had turned around at this moment and looked into Rita's suitcase, he'd have gone into shock!

"All this is yours?" I asked, amazed. "You use this stuff?"

"Sure, you know, it's just shampoo, perfume, makeup, that kind of thing." Rita picked up what looked like a thick rose-colored pen and closed the suitcase lid. "Is this the greatest color? Rainbow Pink."

"You brought markers?"

"This is a nail wand," Rita said as if I should have known. "Look." She twisted off the gold cap and showed me the sparkly pink tip. "It's polish. Want to try some?"

"Okay," I said.

Rita took my hand and began stroking Rainbow Pink over my jaggedy nails.

"What's that smell?" my dad asked, peering back to check on us. "It's overpowering the new car smell!"

"Nail polish," Rita told him.

"Oh," he said, with a strange look on his face. "Well, just be very careful not to spill it."

"It's a polish wand," said Rita with some pride. "It's spill proof."

When my nails were painted, I held them up and fanned them in the air to dry. I stared out the window at the telephone poles whizzing by along Interstate 55. A series of billboards up ahead advertised Ozark Deer Park, where you could pet tame deer and feed them special food, right out of your hand. Maybe we could stop there on the way to Ironvale.

"Hey, Rita, look." I pointed to the billboards.

Rita looked. "So?"

"Oh, nothing," I said, suddenly feeling very babyish for having thought that petting deer would be fun.

"Want me to do your nails?" I asked Rita.

"All right," she said.

I took the nail wand and began applying it to Rita's shapely nails, which looked as if they had about ten coats of Rainbow Pink on them already. I'd never used a nail wand before, so I wasn't very good at it.

I noticed that I was getting polish on Rita's skin along the sides of her nails. Rita noticed too.

"Lila!" she said. "Be more careful!"

Gripping the wand tightly, I began painting her right pinkie, trying my best to keep the polish on the nail. Maybe the car hit a pothole or maybe it didn't, but somehow the wand lurched forward and I found myself painting Rita's knuckle.

"I can't believe this!" Rita jerked her hand away and rummaged through her Samsonite. She came up with a large bottle of yellow polish remover.

"Sorry," I told her. "It slipped."

Rita unscrewed the lid from the polish remover and then took a Beauty Puff and held it over the mouth of the bottle. She turned the bottle upside down, soaked the puff, and then turned the bottle right side up again and held it between her knees as she swiped at the polish I'd gotten on her finger.

I stared nervously at the open bottle.

"Whew!" said my dad from the front seat. "We need some fresh air in here." He rolled down his window.

It must have been the sudden gust of hot wind that did it—that surprised Rita into relaxing her knees and dropping the bottle. Polish remover began pouring all over the carpet on the backseat floor.

Quickly Rita tried to tilt the bottle up with her foot as she reached down to pick it up, but the bottle rolled off the tip of her sandal and slid underneath the front seat, spilling all the way.

"What's going on back there, girls?" My mother began cranking down her window. "I smell polish remover!"

I stared at the dark wet stain on the car rug. If that stuff will take off several coats of Rainbow Pink, I thought, what's it going to do to blue carpet? Boy! When I'd picked out someone to drive my parents crazy, I sure had picked a winner.

"Dad," I said, "have we got any paper towels?"

"No," he said, quickly handing me a box of tissues. "What happened?"

"Oh, I'm sorry!" Rita wailed. "It was an accident!"

Her big eyes filled with tears. She put her head down on her lap, took hold of her knees, and began crying, hard.

"Rita," I said, "don't cry!"

"What's going on?" my mom said, keeping her eyes on the road. "Shall I pull over?"

"Good idea," said my dad.

My mom pulled the car over to the side of the highway and parked. Then both my parents got out of the car. My dad opened Rita's door, and my mom stooped down and put an arm around Rita to comfort her.

"Polish remover," my mom said. "That's what spilled, isn't it?"

Rita's head, still buried in her lap, nodded up and down.

"Listen, Rita," said my mom, "the worst it can do is take some of the coloring out of the rug. There'll be a bleached-out stain. But it's only the floor of a car, for goodness sakes! It's no big tragedy, Rita, okay?"

But Rita just kept sobbing. "It . . . it . . . was an accident! Please!"

"Of course it was." My mom helped Rita out of the car while my dad and I sopped up some of the polish remover with tissues.

As he worked, my dad turned to Rita. "You know, some Native Americans, when they made rugs, always put in a mistake, a little flaw, so that the rug wouldn't be perfect."

This seemed like a strange time for my dad to be telling Indian legends, but at least he got Rita to stop crying for a minute and look at him.

"You see," he went on, "they believed that the gods would be offended if people made anything perfect. They believed only the gods could create something perfect."

Rita looked down at the backseat floor.

"So now our rug has a flaw in it," he went on. "It isn't perfect anymore. Now the gods won't be jealous of our new car." He finished his story and smiled at Rita.

"My daddy would kill me if I did this to his car," she said in a shaky voice. "Really kill me."

My mom gave Rita a last little squeeze and said, "Well, it's all over now. Let's just forget about it."

I wondered if it would be that easy to forget. As long as we had noses, we'd remember.

"On to Ironvale!" said my father, and we climbed into the car, rolled down all the windows, and started off.

"The ants go marching four by four, hurrah! Hurrah!" sang my father as we pulled back out onto the highway.

"The ants go marching four by four," joined in my mother.

"Hurrah! Hurrah!"

For some reason, at that moment I didn't wish that the two crazy people singing in the front seat had found me on their doorstep anymore. I chimed in:

> *"The ants go marching four by four*
> *The little one stops to shut the door . . .*

I looked over at Rita and there she was, eyes red and tearstains still on her cheeks, trying to sing along:

> *". . . And they all go marching down*
> *To the ground*
> *To get out*
> *of the rain*
> *Boom, Boom, BOOM!"*

HOW TO MAKE A BIG IMPRESSION

I took a step back from the small round mirror that hung by a nail over the bathroom sink. The reflection I saw didn't look much like me. Rita had pulled my hair back into a ponytail and tied it with a pink bow. I wondered if the ponytail was supposed to be so tight. It was pulling my eyes over to the sides of my head!

I took another step back from the mirror. Was this really my body inside Rita's lace-trimmed purple T-shirt and pink denim miniskirt? I tried to stand up tall, shoulders back, to be worthy of the new image. It was me, Lila Fenwick, ex-Minnow.

After stopping for a hike through Elephant Rock State Park and a late lunch at the Blue Haven Diner, we'd arrived at Boy Scout camp that afternoon. As our car pulled into the Ironvale parking lot, Rita began tightening her ponytail, brushing it into a perfect plume. "It never hurts to make a good first impression," she'd confided.

I'd looked down at my zoo T-shirt, with a splotch of ketchup from lunch on the chimpanzee's cheek, and at the Band-Aids stretched over each of my knees. It wasn't hard to figure out what kind of first impression I'd make: awful! Could even Rita Morgan transform me with some S.O.S.? She certainly had her work cut out for her.

Now Rita and I were getting ourselves all ready to impress the Boy Scouts of America at our first dinner at Ironvale. We were taking turns looking in the mirror in the bathroom of our cabin, the Health Lodge.

HEALTH LODGE. That's what the dark wooden letters on our building said, but it seemed to me they should say SICK LODGE, since it was the camp infirmary. My dad had told us there was only one patient there now, a Boy Scout with the stomach flu.

The medical staff stayed in the back half of the Health Lodge. My mom and dad had a room next to the bathroom and across a narrow pine-paneled hallway from the rooms where Grace Lindquist and her kids stayed. Rita and I were supposed to share a tiny closet of a room next door to the nurse's quarters, but instead we had pulled our bunks onto the large cool screened-in porch that ran along the back of the building.

"My turn," announced Rita as she stepped in front of me at the mirror, turning up the collar of her pale peach blouse just so and centering the dainty pink shell she wore on a silver chain around her neck. After a moment of silent admiration, she pulled herself away from the mirror and inspected me briefly.

"We look like a million dollars!" Rita declared. "For real!"

"Thanks again for letting me wear this outfit," I told her. I hoped I wouldn't spill anything on it at dinner.

"Time for some Icy Peach!" Rita pulled a golden lipstick case from her makeup pouch. "Ooo doough," Rita went on, her mouth half open and her lips stretched tight across her teeth as she glided on her Icy Peach, "iss wary ihortant ho hake a hig hurst ihmhression."

"What??"

Rita pressed her glossy lips together on a square of toilet paper. "I said it's very important to make a big first impression."

"Yeah, you mentioned that," I told her.

"If you don't make a big impression—right away—a boy is going to take one look at you and that's it. You're over."

Unless you look like somebody's third grade sister, I thought.

"Here," she said, handing me another lipstick. "Frosty Rose. Try it."

Rita was taking to her role as my S.O.S. teacher

like a duck to water—and I hadn't even asked her to do it! I pulled off the lipstick top, rolled up the pink tip, and rubbed it on my lips. Then I pressed my lips together on some T.P. as I had seen Rita do.

I popped the top back on the lipstick and was about to hand it to Rita when she shrieked, "Lila! You didn't roll it down!"

I pulled off the top of the Frosty Rose and saw what she meant. What had once been a shapely pink point was now a smashed pink mess.

"Oh, no!" I cried. "I'm really sorry!"

"Never mind." Rita shrugged. "You keep that one."

Pocketing my first lipstick, I pulled the string that turned off the bare bulb over the bathroom sink. Then Rita and I walked back to the porch, where my mom and dad were waiting for us so that we could all go to dinner together.

When my father saw us coming, he said, "All ready to . . ." That was as far as he got. After that his mouth closed and he just stared.

"Ta dah!" I said, turning around for him, like a model. "How do you like my new look?"

"Keep looking," my dad muttered.

My mom was staring, too, especially at my lips. "Well," she finally managed, "shall we escort you two ladies to the formal dining room?"

My mom and dad walked ahead of Rita and me on Red Rock Trail up to the Dining Hall. Rita talked to me a mile a minute, while my parents walked most of the way in silence. But once I heard my dad say to my mom, "Didn't anyone tell those two that this was a *camping* trip?"

"I'd like to welcome all our new campers to Ironvale!" The voice of Shepherd Dorty, the camp director, boomed out over the P.A. system in the Dining Hall. "In a day or two you new-timers will feel like old-timers."

Rita and I were sitting on a bench next to my mom and dad at a long wooden table known as Doc's Table because one end of it was reserved for the camp doctor and nurse and their families. The Lindquists, who had already been at camp for two weeks, had gone into Ironton this evening to take in a movie and a bit of "civilization," my dad said. The rest of our table was occupied by the overflow from Troop 97.

My dad had us all introduce ourselves.

"Schwimm," the boy sitting across from me had said. "Sinker Schwimm." White white scalp beamed through the bristles of his quarter-inch haircut. Badges lined his chest like a general's.

"Rusty Hart," said the boy next to him, who had carrot-colored hair. He had a pen and was doodling on his napkin, a picture of a rattlesnake coiled to strike.

"Fox James."

"Mac Wolken."

And so on and so on, down one side of the table and up the other. None of the Scouts in Troop 97 had names like John or Christopher. They were all Buzzy and Tork, Wimpy and Bonkers.

"Old-timers," Shepherd Dorty was saying into the mike, "let's welcome the new Scouts with the camp song. Ready?"

> *"Over hill, over dale,*
> *Pack our horse and hit the trail,*
> *From Camp Ironvale we all love so well;*
> *On the run, games and fun,*
> *And "Be Prepared" till day is done,*
> *At Camp Ironvale we all love so well."*

At the end there was wild applause.

"Very good, campers!" Shep Dorty said. "Excellent. Now I have some people to introduce. First, we have with us a Scout who began coming to Ironvale when he was ten years old. I know, because he was my first bunk mate. He went on to achieve Order of the Arrow as well as Eagle Scout and he'll be here with us for the next two weeks as camp doctor, so take a good look at him when he stands up, boys, and you'll know who to see if you decide to add poison ivy to your leaf collections. Dr. Philip Fenwick!"

My father rose, smiling, and gave a Scout salute. "We're happy to be back at Ironvale," he said, "and we hope we won't see most of you over at the Health Lodge. If you can remember this one bit of advice, chances are we won't: Leaves of three—let it be!" He sat back down.

"And," continued Shep Dorty, "Dr. Fenwick has brought his family along with him. Please welcome Mrs. Fenwick, their daughter, Lila, and her friend Rita."

My mom stood up halfway out of her chair and gave a little wave. I copied what she did, trying to smile. But Rita sprang up from her chair and waved as if she were riding on a float in the Rose Bowl Parade.

"All right!" a boy at a faraway table shouted into the big room.

"Va-va-voom!" another Scout called out, setting off a wave of similar comments.

Rita had made a big first impression all right. It occurred to me then that with Rita around all the time to make such a big impression, I might not make any impression at all. Zero. Lila Fenwick: Invisible Girl.

Only when Shep began his announcements of the morning's schedule did Rita sit back down.

"The Polar Bears will meet at the swimming hole at the far end of Red Rock Trail for their prebreakfast swim starting tomorrow at 6:30 A.M. sharp. If you show up every morning and actually take a dip, no matter what the temperature, at the end of camp you will be initiated into the Royal Order of the Polar Bear. We usually have a dozen or so Scouts who become Polar Bears. It's a great honor but, unfortunately, it's not a regulation merit badge."

Shep said some more stuff about safety at the

archery range and times for swimming tests and tonight's big campfire. He ended his announcements with, "Let's sing grace, campers."

With the last note of "amen," there was a mad scramble as two servers from each table speed-walked to the front of the Dining Hall, grabbed up big brown trays, and slid them along as cafeteria workers put on bowls of food for them to take back to their tables. My dad and the boy with the basic training hair had volunteered to be the servers from our table. "It beats clearing," Sinker said.

As we waited for our food, Rita nudged me.

"Lila!" she whispered. "There's this totally T.K.O. boy at the next table. Facing us. With real short hair. See him?"

Rita's description could have fit any of several dozen boys at the tables around ours. I looked without finding the boy she meant, but when I turned back to her, Rita seemed to have found another totally T.K.O. boy in a more convenient location.

"This place," Rita was saying to Rusty Hart, "is like so natural, you know?"

"I guess." Rusty kept doodling.

Rita beamed her baby blues full on this Scout and began her work. "It's such an enormous place! I don't think I'll ever learn my way around here!"

"It's big," replied Rusty, "but it isn't hard to get around. The trails are all marked with rocks, different colors. Red Rock's the main trail, then there's

Black Rock, White Rock, and Speckled Rock. Once you figure it out, you can't get lost."

"Get lost!" Rita shivered. "Don't even say that! Are the woods full of any, you know, wild animals?"

"You mean," Rusty slowly raised his snake-filled napkin and held it in front of Rita's face, "like this?"

Rita gave a little screech and then glared at Rusty just as Sinker, holding a large dented aluminum pitcher, turned her glass right side up and said, "Bug juice?"

"What!?" shrieked Rita.

"It's fruit punch," my mom reassured her. "They just call it bug juice to be funny."

Meanwhile my dad returned from the cafeteria line and began passing out serving dishes of meat loaf, mashed potatoes, gravy, peas, and corn bread.

"Here, Rita," he said, handing her a platter. "Have some mystery meat."

"No thanks," Rita huffed, taking the dish with her fingertips and quickly passing it to me.

The way things were going, I didn't think Rita's mother would have to worry about her gaining weight.

That night, as Rita and I lay in our bunks, arranged head to head on the screened-in porch of the Health Lodge, we listened to the sounds of nature. It seemed to me that someone ought to turn down the volume!

Jug-o-rum! Jug-o-rum! My dad had told us those were

bullfrogs. *Tungh! Tungh! Tungh!* He'd said these were the calls of the green frogs. Even I knew the crickets. *Churrrrrip! Churrrrrip!* They sounded like telephones ringing in the distance. Then I heard the worst sound of them all: *Zzzzzzzzzz*, the buzzing mosquito, invisible in the night. And even worse than its whine was its silence while I worried that, somewhere on my body, it was sucking my blood.

"I don't think I'll *ever* go to sleep out here!" complained Rita from her bunk. "Listen to those horrible toads!"

"Frogs," I said.

"I swear, I think we should move our beds back inside! Listen!"

A ghostly *ooooooooo-oooooo* echoed through the trees.

"What was *that?*" Rita pulled her blanket up to her chin. "Lila, I'm not kidding, I can't stay out here! I'll never be able to sleep!"

"Don't worry," I told her. "It's probably an owl. They hunt at night. Maybe they like the full moon or something." I stopped to listen and heard the owl, closer now. "But an owl couldn't get in here," I told Rita. "We've got the screens to protect us. Nothing can get in. Okay?"

There was silence.

"Rita?"

I heard a snuffling sound. I stopped talking and listened. There it was again and this time I identified it—Rita was snoring!

I lay in my bunk waiting for sleep too. *Jug-o-rum.*
Jug-o-rum. Tungh. Tungh. Tungh. Ooooooo! Ooooooo!
And then—*BONG! BONG! BONG!*

I sat straight up in my bunk. That was *not* a sound
of nature. Somebody—or something—was right outside! It didn't sound like a Boy Scout with the stomach flu. Could it be a raccoon robbing the garbage
can?

BONG! BONG!

Then I heard a voice. I couldn't make out what it
was saying, but it didn't sound happy. What if it
was some crazy hermit from the woods?

"Rita!" I whispered loudly. But only her snore answered me.

I was curious, but there was no way I was going
outside to investigate. I grabbed my specs and my
flashlight and then tiptoed silently to the corner of
the porch. Aiming my flashlight out through the
screen, I clicked it on.

"Cut it out!" came a harsh voice.

But I didn't move. In my beam of light stood a
girl! A girl in a plaid shirt and jeans. Could this be
Kari Lindquist? She didn't look old enough to be in
high school as she stood beside an enormous rusty
trash can, her arms folded angrily across her chest
and her head turned away to keep the light out of
her eyes.

"Turn that light off!" The girl spun and squinted
straight into the flashlight beam. Her small face had
a sharp little nose and her eyes practically sizzled

with anger. She had short blond hair that stuck up in tufts like some badly clipped bush. As I watched, she pulled back her leg and kicked the trash can for all she was worth. *BONG!*

I clicked off my flashlight. Rita's regular breathing told me that somehow she had slept through the banging, but there was no way I could get to sleep now. I threw on a long sweat shirt and went outside to see what in the world was going on.

"Get out of here!" the girl said as I walked toward her. She was almost as short as I was, but not as skinny. "Beat it!"

I stopped where I was. "What am I supposed to do, try to sleep with you kicking that thing? What are you doing out here anyway?"

"None of your beeswax!" Her voice was low and gravelly. She gave the can another loud kick—and no wonder it was so loud. She was wearing pointy-toed cowboy boots! Then in a burst of anger she lunged at the can with her shoulder, shoving it to the ground. Trash spewed everywhere onto the dirt. At first the girl just stared at the mess, and then she went over to a piece of wadded-up tissue and pressed it with the toe of her boot. She pressed a few more tissues this way and then got mad again and started stomping on them and kicking the overturned trash can. *BONG! BONG!*

"Wait a second! Wait a second!" I told her between kicks. "I get it. You lost something, right? And you think it might have gotten thrown in the trash?"

"I bet you get all *A*'s in school!" The girl gave the can one more hard bang and flopped down, sitting on a tree stump off to the side of her trash pile. She sighed loudly and then said to me in a voice that wasn't so angry anymore, "Who are you, anyway?"

"Lila," I told her, "Lila Fenwick."

"The doctor's kid."

"Right," I said. "You're Kari Lindquist?"

She nodded.

"I think our parents have been friends forever," I began. "I think my dad and your dad—"

BONG! Kari was up and kicking again. *BONG!* I guessed she didn't want me to talk about her father.

"Uh . . . " I didn't know what to say now. "You're in high school?"

"Eighth grade."

"I'm going into sixth," I told her before she had a chance to guess fourth.

Kari surveyed the trash in silence.

"So you're staying at the Health Lodge too?" I asked.

"All summer, every summer," she said.

"Every summer!" I was impressed. "Are you usually the only girl here?"

"Sometimes." She shrugged as if it didn't really matter much to her and kicked at a paper cup.

"So what's in here," I asked, "that's so important? Your diamond necklace?"

That got a smile out of Kari, and I saw that one of

her front teeth overlapped the other in a way that made her smile sort of pointy. I liked it right away.

"My retainer," she said. "I took it out this afternoon while I was eating a bag of chips. I always wrap it in a tissue while I eat 'cause it looks, you know, so gross. Then I guess I tossed it into the trash with the empty bag."

"Tossed it," I echoed, looking with new meaning at the little white wads on the ground.

Kari looked grimly at the scattered trash. "So I guess I've got to dig through here."

If ever a girl needed a Great Idea, it was Kari.

"Let me think," I told her. The trash wasn't only trash, but garbage too. Banana peels. Bits of hamburger bun. *Dis*-gusting! "If only you didn't have to touch all the guck."

"That would help."

"Your mom's the nurse," I said, thinking aloud. And then I smiled. "I've got a Great Idea how we could do it."

"We?" Kari looked surprised.

"Come on," I told her. "First we have to raid the Health Lodge."

Ten minutes later Kari and I pushed open the screen door and crept down the flagstone steps from the Health Lodge toward the trash. During our absence a raccoon had discovered the easy-to-get-to tidbits. It was sitting in the midst of the mess, feasting. But the raccoon took one look at us, gave a little yelp of surprise, and hurtled back into the woods. And no wonder! We looked a little strange.

I had only meant to borrow some disposable gloves from the examining room of the Health Lodge. But as we shone our flashlights around in search of the gloves, we had found a few other pieces of protective clothing that we decided to use as well. We had tucked our hair out of the way into green paper caps, the kinds that doctors wear in the operating room. I couldn't imagine why these caps were even at the Health Lodge, since it didn't have an operating room, but they were. Over our clothes we wore long white paper gowns that tied in the back and covered us from our chins to the ground. We'd had to roll up the long sleeves so our hands would stick out. On our hands we'd put the plastic gloves. And when we found the surgical masks, we'd decided that they might cut down on the garbage smell. We'd tied those on too. And so we came, like very short surgeons, into the moonlit night.

"Let's get organized!" My voice was muffled by the mask. "Why don't we dump what's left out of the can and then we can throw it back in as we go through the trash?"

"Sounds good to me, Dr. Fenwick," said Kari. "Let's operate."

"After you, Dr. Lindquist," I replied.

We began picking up the little white wads, pressing them, and tossing them back in the trash can.

"This is slimy work," I said, giggling. "Even with all this protection."

"So quit," said Kari. "I *have* to do this. You don't."

"What? Quit in the middle of an operation? Hey!" I called. "I think I've got it!"

I scraped some gooey tissue aside, and there in my hand lay a peach pit.

"Good try, Dr. Fenwick," said Kari. "Wait a minute. Did you hear that?"

I stood still. Twigs snapped behind me. I turned, but I couldn't see anything in the woods. "Think it's that raccoon?"

"Probably." Kari shrugged and we went back to work. Pick up, press, toss. Pick up, press, toss. Pick up, press, toss. Nothing.

"It's a good thing there's a full moon," I said, glancing up at Kari. But Kari wasn't picking up, pressing, and tossing anymore. She was staring wide-eyed at something in back of me. I twisted my head around and saw why: Behind me stood three Boy Scouts.

"What's going on here?" I recognized that voice. Was it Sinker from the Dining Hall? One Scout shone a flashlight directly at us.

The circle of light revealed Kari standing there in her paper gown, a mask over the bottom half of her face, like some demented doctor from a bad dream. I started laughing the weird nervous kind of laugh that I wasn't sure I could stop. How were we going to explain this? Then I knew. We weren't.

Ducking my head down, I tried to talk like a boy. "Had a little accident out here. We're with the Night Cleanup Patrol."

"Oouugh," the middle Boy Scout moaned. I saw that he was wearing pajamas.

"Night Cleanup?" asked one of the other Scouts.

Where had I heard that voice? I peeked up at him and my heart nearly stopped. I hoped my eyes were playing tricks on me, because if they weren't, then I was looking right into the face of T.K.O. Hans Pearson! Hans! Coach's Diving Daredevil! Here? Was *this* the counselor's job he'd mentioned that day at N.A.P.? Ironvale?"

"That's right," Kari was saying, making her voice even gravellier than it was. "Night Cleanup."

"I . . . I'm gonna be sick again," groaned the pajamaed Scout.

"Okay," said Hans. "Sinker, take Mac on into the Health Lodge. Go around to the front. I'll be there in a sec." He turned back to us. "What troop are you two with?"

"Troop 4," I said, at exactly the same time Kari said, "Troop 6."

"Different troops," I said gruffly. Then I stepped as far away from Hans as I could get, bent down, and started working on the trash again, hoping he'd go away.

But he didn't go away. I could hear his steps coming closer and closer and closer. My heart was racing like a marathon runner's. Why was he coming over to me? I couldn't stand it!

I stood up fast and faced him, yanking down my mask. "I know, I know," I said, using my own voice once again. "I look very familiar, right?"

"Yeah . . . " Hans began, looking puzzled, and then he broke out one of his crooked smiles. "Lila Fenwick!" he said. "I couldn't believe it when I saw you get introduced at dinner tonight."

Well, at least he remembers me, I thought.

Kari lowered her mask. "Hi, Hans," she said.

"Hi, Kar," he answered.

It sounded like they knew each other pretty well. I wondered if Hans was Kari's boyfriend.

"But what are you doing out here?" Hans gestured toward the trash. "Dressed up like . . . like Halloween?"

"I threw out my retainer," explained Kari, "by accident, and it's got to be in here someplace, so we're hunting for it and trying to protect ourselves from the goo."

Hans shook his head. "Good luck."

"Don't you want to help?" I asked him. "It could be your good deed for the day."

"Thanks anyway," said Hans, backing away from us. "I've got to go see how Mac is doing. He made a bet with his bunk mate that he could drink three pitchers of bug juice at dinner, and he isn't feeling too great."

"Three pitchers!" The thought of it almost made me sick.

Hans waved. "Later!"

I turned back to Kari. She had a weird look on her face.

"What's the matter?" I asked her.

Kari was pressing her side, the way you do when your stomach hurts and you're trying to see if it's appendicitis. Then she reached under her surgical gown into a small pocket of her jeans and pulled out a pink plastic roof of a mouth surrounded by a single silver wire.

"It was in your *pocket?*" I said. "The whole time?"

Kari just stared at me and nodded.

"Then all this . . ." I looked at the mess surrounding us. "Oh, no!" We started laughing like lunatics!

"I'll put the rest of the garbage back in myself," said Kari, catching her breath.

"Forget it," I told her. "Let's just see how fast the Night Cleanup Patrol can get it all back in."

We picked up the trash. No more pressing, just scoop and toss as fast as we could. While I worked, my mind replayed what had just happened. Why Hans? Why tonight? Why did he have to see me looking so ridiculous? At least it wasn't a first impression. I'd already made that by looking like Jeannie Jansey. And it wasn't even a second impression, which I'd already made by splatting down the steps at N.A.P.—ka-boom! But this was a big impression—Dr. Lila "Trash" Fenwick. Beneath my mask a small smile appeared as I thought about it. Even Rita would have to agree with me—I'd be hard to forget.

HOW TO
FIND THE TRUE YOU

Wuck-a-wuck-a-wuck-a.

"Listen! That's him!" My mom halted, still as a statue, on the trail. Rita and I, walking behind her, just about knocked her over when she stopped so suddenly like that, but she hardly noticed. Her eyes searched the branches above our heads. At last she looked down again and gave a disgusted huff. "I've been listening to this woodpecker all week and haven't seen so much as a feather! I think he's invisible!"

We began walking again, up to the Dining Hall for breakfast. It was the beginning of day six at Ironvale and, in my opinion, everything had gone wrong, starting the first morning we woke up here. It had been nothing but *yuck-a-yuck-a-yuck-a*.

"What happens when you see the woodpecker, Mrs. Fenwick?" Rita asked.

"Then I get to mark 'Pileated Woodpecker' on my life list," answered my mom.

"That's it?" asked Rita. "You write his name on a list?"

"It doesn't sound too exciting when you put it like that, does it?" My mom chuckled.

"What do you get if you have the longest list?" asked Rita.

"You get the pleasure of having identified the most birds," my mom said.

"You don't get anything?" asked Rita. "Isn't there a prize for seeing the pileated woodpecker?"

I'd never been that big on birding myself, but to Rita it was a total mystery. She seemed to think it was like a contest or a TV quiz show. I think Rita wanted to picture my mom on "Birding for Dollars," winning a year's supply of Birds Eye frozen string beans for seeing the yellow-bellied sapsucker or a Thunderbird convertible for spotting a red-tailed hawk! I didn't think my mom would ever be able to explain the joys of birding to Rita.

As we got close to the Dining Hall, I saw Kari waiting by the door. She waved. Rita waved back, but I barely raised a finger. I couldn't even look at Kari without feeling hurt, left out, and angry. I thought back to the night I'd met Kari playing kick-the-trash-can in her cowboy boots, mad as a hornet. She'd seemed like a real tomboy. I'd worried that she and Miss Perfect would be enemies at first sight, and I'd even tried to dream up some Great Ideas for helping the three of us strays get along. I shouldn't have bothered. The two of them got along just fine.

The morning after the missing retainer episode, right after reveille, Kari had come out to the porch dressed in a red flannel shirt and jeans. Her hair seemed to have sprouted a few more branches in the night, and it didn't look as if Kari had tried to brush them out. I'd introduced her to Rita, who was already up and at 'em in a pink-and-white terry cloth shorts outfit, and when Rita found out that Kari had been coming to Ironvale every summer for years, Rita got *very* interested.

"So," she'd said, "what do you do around here?"

"What I do is ride Rocky," Kari had said, her face lighting up as she spoke. "He's like my own horse. I'm only supposed to get him when the boys don't have riding, but Charlie—he's in charge at the stables—Charlie never minds if I keep him out."

"You ride at the same time the Scouts are riding?" asked Rita. "Same trails?"

Kari nodded. "Rocky's the best horse in the world. And Ginger—she's great too. Want to go see them?"

"I'd *love* to!" gushed Rita. "I just adore horses!"

With that the two of them ran out the door of the Health Lodge, leaving me sitting on my bunk in my pajamas wondering how it was that Rita Morgan, who hated just about everything that had to do with animals and nature, liked horses. How could I have guessed that someone who thought guinea pigs were disgusting would be crazy for big toothy animals that had flies buzzing around their eyes? Maybe her ponytail should have given me a clue. But the minute Rita'd said giddyup to some fleabag horse, she'd said whoa to my lessons in S.O.S.

Woe—that was the story of my life. Kari and Rita went off to the stables right after breakfast every day and just came back for lunch and dinner.

At first they tried to talk me into going riding with them.

"Try it once!" urged Kari. "Just sit on a horse. You'll love it!"

"If only the pain in my knees wasn't so horrible!" I lied dramatically, remembering how it felt to be upside down under that pony.

"It's only swimming you're not allowed to do," Miss Perfect Rita reminded me. "Anyway, riding is no big deal. You just have to show a horse who's boss. Don't you want to even come look at Rocky and Ginger? They are soooo gorgeous!"

"No thanks," I said.

"Lightning's really gentle with beginners," said Kari.

"Lightning?" I said. "Not a chance."

"So what are you gonna do?" Rita asked me.

I shrugged. "Go birding with my mom, I guess," I said, because that's about all there was left for me to do, since swimming was out and the only other strays at Ironvale this season were Kari's little brothers.

Rita looked suspicious. "Just you and your mom?"

"Yeah," I said, "what do you think? We invited the loons in Troop 97?"

Rita hadn't said anything more about birding until this morning, on the trail. But just before she and Kari left for the stables after breakfast, Rita turned to me.

"You know something, Lila?" she said, tightening the rubber band that held her ponytail high on her head, "if you're not careful, you're going to turn into one of those bird nerds."

Those bird nerds. I knew who she meant. Lonely people who tramp around in the woods and fields, cameras and binoculars clanking around their necks, slim books sticking out of every pocket, walking briskly as they tote little canvas stools on the ends of pointed sticks that they stab into the ground when they're ready for a rest.

The awful thing was, in my heart I knew that Rita had hit upon a grain of truth. Deep down inside, the true me probably *was* a bird nerd, trying desperately not to be by putting on nail polish and lipstick, borrowing lacy outfits, and trying to learn the S.O.S. I was beginning to doubt whether a pigeon ever could turn into a peacock—or the Mighty Minnow into a Mermaid.

Half an hour after breakfast, my mom and I were on Speckled Rock Trail, stalking the wild woodpecker. My mom had shown me a picture of it in my *Field Guide to Birds*—the pileated woodpecker, a huge Woody Woodpecker look-alike, mostly black with white markings on its neck and face and this enormous red crest on top of its head. It seemed as if it would be hard *not* to spot this bird, but it was very skillful at hiding. Even though my mom could hear its call, she could never catch a glimpse of it. It was driving her cuckoo!

Wuck-a-wuck-a-wuck-a.

"Do you hear it, Lila?" my mom whispered. "Do you?"

"Loud and clear," I told her.

"This bird is wearing me out!" she said, sitting down on a wooden bench beside the trail and doing a few neck circles. "Why is it so hard to get a look at him?"

I didn't have the answer to that one. I didn't seem to have the answer to much these days.

"Mom," I began, plopping down next to her and taking an apple from my backpack, "when you were growing up, did you ever feel, well, different from your friends or anything? Like when you were about my age?"

"Let me think back," said my mom. She put her feet up on a stump near the bench. "When I was eleven, going into sixth grade? No, I don't think so, Lila."

Well, I thought, biting into my apple, it's just me.

"No," my mom went on, almost as if she were talking to herself now. "It wasn't until I was in junior high that I started feeling different."

"You did?" I asked. "How?"

"I was what my mother used to call a late bloomer," she said.

"You mean you looked . . . younger than your friends?"

"Have I ever shown you my eighth grade homeroom picture?" she asked. "Three rows of kids that all look about the same age and then, right in the front row, it looks like there's a visitor from grade school. That was me. I look about four years younger than anyone else."

I thought about this information as I crunched on my apple. On the one hand, it was good news that my mom had gone through what I was going through and she had turned out to be a more or less normal person. On the other hand, maybe I would look and feel this way for another three or four years! That thought was horrifying!

"Your father too," my mom went on. "Talk about late bloomers. It isn't everyone who keeps going to Boy Scout camp all the way through medical school! And when he opened his office, his first patients couldn't believe he was a real doctor because he looked so young." My mom gave me a half smile. "I'm afraid you come from a long line of late bloomers," she said, "but it doesn't have to be such a bad thing. When all your friends are old and gray, you'll still look like a spring chicken!"

It was little comfort that I'd have the last laugh in thirty-five years!

"It's just that everyone around me is changing," I told my mom. "Starting to go crazy over boys, getting, you know, to look . . . older." I cupped my hands and held them way out in front of my nonexistent breasts. "I just wonder when it's going to be my turn."

"Everyone has her own timetable for developing physically," answered my mom.

I hated it when my mom used words like *developing* and *physically*. I hoped I hadn't gotten her started on anything that would lead her to talk to me about getting my period, which, since she'd been taking those courses at her college, she called *men-struuuuu-a-shun*.

"You really can't do anything to hurry it up," she was saying, "so you might as well relax and enjoy being who you are at eleven. Don't worry, honey. Your turn will come."

I looked down and saw that the big scab on my right knee was about to fall off. I thought about asking my mom if she had been clumsy when she was young, but I couldn't bear the thought that she might say yes. I didn't want to hear that I came from a long line of klutzes.

Above my head a lone bird called out into the quickly fading summer morning. *Burrrrr! Burrrrr!* As

I listened, the call seemed to turn into Rita's warning: *Birrrrrd! Nerrrrrrrd!* That's me, I thought, the brown-headed late-blooming bird nerd.

Another chirper joined the first, but this one's call was different. *True you! True you! True you!* it sang.

Okay, birds. I get the message.

Maybe the true me is a bird nerd, I thought. Is that so terrible? My father always says, "Lila, you can be whatever you want to be—but be a good one." Well, I could be a birder and a good one too. I could spot more birds than anyone. Maybe I'd even see a bird no one has ever seen before, lurking deep in the Ironvale woods, and maybe it'd be named after me: Fenwick's Flycatcher.

After my little talk with myself I began thinking about birding with a new enthusiasm. I tossed my apple core and opened my little green birding book. I saw that already this week my life list of four birds had grown to more than twenty. Just this morning I'd seen a pair of flickers, a thrasher, some finches, and a grackle. A family of bobwhites had scurried across the trail, right in front of our feet, and, skulking at the top of a tree, I'd seen a buzzard.

It was thinking about how I'd felt when I saw the buzzard that did it—that made me understand that, strange as it seemed, I liked looking up in a tree and seeing a big old bald-headed turkey buzzard more than I liked looking at myself in the mirror. And I realized that just as it would be impossible for my mom to explain birding to Rita, it would be equally impossible for Rita to teach me the Secrets of Sophistication. If the S.O.S. were all about makeup and clothes, I didn't really want to know about them anyway.

Forget S.O.S., I thought. Now I had a truly Great Idea: I'd become Lila Fenwick, Birding Ace.

"Lila," my mom said, finishing a set of pushups she'd been doing against the bench and looking at her watch. "I promised Grace Lindquist I'd relieve her at the infirmary for an hour this morning so she could take the twins into town to get them some fishing gear. I think we'd better start back."

"But we've just gone halfway down this trail," I complained. I couldn't let my birding career come to an end before it had even started. "Can't I keep going by myself?"

"You really shouldn't be in the woods alone, Lila," my mom said.

"I'll stay on Speckled Rock Trail," I told her. "It's just that we've come so close to the woodpecker and I'm not ready to give up on seeing him yet. Please!"

My mom beamed me a smile that made it perfectly clear that she was thrilled to have a bird nerd for a daughter. "Well," she said, "I guess it'll be okay. But don't go off the trail."

"I won't," I told her. "See you at lunch. Wuck-a-wuck-a!"

My feet crunched on the dry pine needles of Speckled Rock Trail. It forked to the left, the right fork being marked with big white stones. I didn't know just where Speckled Rock led, but it was bound to lead somewhere. And, as my dad always said, You're never lost if you don't care where you are.

In the trees above I heard the scolding of a sparrow. I walked on, and at a turn in the path I noticed that the trees began to grow thicker, letting less light onto the trail. I passed a cluster of orange mushrooms sprouting from a rotten stump. Just as I was wondering if I should turn back to the more well lit section of the trail, I heard a distant *wuck-a-wuck-a-wuck-a*.

I froze in my tracks, as I had seen my mom do, and listened hard. My heart was beating with excitement and I realized that I wanted to see this woodpecker—very much.

The *wuck-a*'s seemed to be coming from my left. Being careful to avoid "leaves of three," I stepped quietly off the trail and into the woods. *Wuck-a-wuck-a-wuck-a.* It was louder now. Taking big slow steps, I moved in the *wuck-a* direction. I'd told my mom I wouldn't go off the trail. But this was only a few steps. And besides, she'd want me to if she thought I could see the woodpecker. I looked up but saw nothing. I moved closer to the last *wuck-a*'s and stopped. Then, not far above my head, I heard *Rat-a-tat! Rat-a-tat!* This was a woodpecker, all right, but where? I took a few more steps toward where I thought the *rat-a-tat*'s had been. Then I looked back to make sure I could still see the trail. I couldn't. Maybe I'd taken more steps than I thought.

I turned in a circle. I felt confused. Now I couldn't tell which direction I'd come from. What if I was lost?

Wuck-a-wuck-a-wuck-a.

Even though my heart was hammering a terrified rat-a-tat-tat louder than any woodpecker's, when I heard another round of *wuck-a*'s, I looked up. Above me I saw the spreading branches of an oak. Those branches gave me an idea. If I could climb high enough in the tree, I'd be able to see the trail.

I plunked my pack at the base of the tree, tucked my binoculars inside my T-shirt to be sure I'd see the trail, and with a small jump grabbed the lowest branch. It was a struggle for me to hold on, walk my feet up the trunk, and hook a leg around the branch, but I did it. From there I kept going up, branch by branch. I couldn't look down. I just kept climbing. The whole time I was scared I'd slip. Why hadn't I stayed on the trail like I'd told my mom I would?

About halfway up the tree, I centered myself on a sturdy branch, hugged the tree trunk, and looked down. So this is a bird's-eye view, I thought, squeezing the trunk more tightly.

The first thing I saw was Eagle Peak. Even though I'd never seen it before, right away I recognized the craggy shape of an eagle's head curving down into a sharp beak. I wondered how the legend had gotten started. I wondered if it could be true. Then and there I promised myself that if I ever got out of that tree and out of those woods alive, I'd go to Eagle Peak and sleep under the stars.

But now I had to find the trail. Gripping the tree trunk with one arm, I pulled out my binoculars and scanned the woods for little paths of brown among the green. I couldn't see any. I guessed that, from the height I was in the tree, the thick undergrowth blocked out the narrow trails. If only someone were walking on the trail, I thought. Then I could tell where it was.

As if in answer to my thoughts, I heard distant voices and the pounding of sneakers on hard-packed dirt. I didn't have to wait long before I saw the heads of a line of Scouts bobbing along a trail, and from the whoops and the wild way they ran, I had a feeling that I was looking at part of Troop 97. I could imagine that birds and squirrels, rabbits and chipmunks were scurrying out of Troop 97's way, just as they fled from the Wicked Queen in Disney's movie, *Snow White*!

As I watched, the Scouts ran to a clearing a stone's throw from my tree and dropped their packs. A few of them picked up fallen branches and sticks and began sword fighting.

"The Ninja never dies!" cried Mac Wolken, doing some kind of karate kick as he whipped his stick sword in a circle above his head.

"The way of the Dragon shall prevail!" Fox James shouted, flipping his branch around as if he were a baton twirler.

"Knock off the Ninja!" To my ears came a voice that I was getting to know all too well. "Let's get this camp set up!"

Oh, great! I thought. For my next big impression I'll be Lila Fenwick, Tree Sitter!

Hans began giving orders. "Kindling, Schwimm and Hart! Firewood, James and Wolken! Marzollo and Osborn, get the water. Let's move!"

The Ninja warriors dropped their weapons and scattered in search of wood or water. Sinker and Rusty dashed into the woods and began checking the area around the base of my tree for kindling. I shut my eyes, afraid that if I watched them, they'd feel it and look up and see me. I wondered what they'd think if they did.

"Whose pack is that?" I heard Sinker say.

My eyes flew open. My pack! I'd forgotten about my pack!

"Guess someone left it here," said Rusty. "We can take it back to camp."

"There any I.D. inside?" asked Sinker.

I heard nothing while they unbuckled my pack and pulled things out. Should I say something, I wondered?

"Lila Fenwick," Sinker said.

"Let's take it," said Rusty. "We can give it to her at dinner."

"Wonder what she was doing out here anyway?" said Sinker.

Just then Hans's voice called, "Hey Hart! Schwimm!

We can't get a fire started without the kindling! Hurry it up!"

Sinker threw my pack over one shoulder and began scurrying around picking up little sticks. Neither he nor Rusty looked up, and when their hands were full they raced back to their clearing.

My branch was beginning to feel hard and scratchy. I wondered if I'd be spotted if I tried to climb down now. I wondered if I could climb down. I scooted into a slightly less uncomfortable position and waited.

Sinker and Rusty were laying their kindling over dry leaves in the pit that Hans had dug for the fire. Mac bent over the kindling, and then Fox appeared with an armload of small logs.

"Mac! Get out of here with that magnifying glass!" shouted Fox.

"Come on!" said Mac. "I just want to try it. If I can direct the sun on this leaf it'll catch fire in a few seconds. Just let me give it a try."

"You already tried it in Joskey's field," said Sinker.

"I didn't start that fire!" Mac yelled at him.

"Let's just get *this* fire started!" barked Hans.

As I watched I thought back to that day at N.A.P., when Gayle and Kelly had been watching Hans. Maybe they had a point. Right now it seemed that boy watching was at least as interesting as bird watching. Maybe this was my chance to add some new names to my life list: the Red-Neckerchiefed Tenderfoot and the Khaki-Chested Eagle Scout!

"Why don't you just rub two sticks together?" Sinker taunted Mac.

"It would take forever!" said Mac.

"Not if one of the sticks was a match!" shouted Sinker.

A round of groans followed Sinker's awful joke.

"Okay," said Hans. "Who's going for the cooking merit badge? Schwimm and Hart, right?"

Sinker and Rusty nodded.

"Better get started then," Hans said. "The rest of you can keep working on your weather badges."

"I think I see some cumulonimbus clouds gathering," announced Fox. "It's gonna rain!"

"Those are altocumulus, cloudhead!" said Mac. "No way for rain!"

Oh, great. The Scouts were going to be looking up at the sky now. I wished I'd worn a bark-colored T-shirt instead of a red one. I remembered Winnie-the-Pooh pretending that he was a little black rain cloud to fool the honeybees. I didn't think I'd be able to fool any of the Scouts. What excuse could I have for being up a tree so close to their clearing?

Before I could even work on a Great Idea for explaining it, I heard that old familiar tune: *wuck-a-wuck-a-wuck-a.* I started to reach for my binoculars, but this time I didn't need them. Almost directly above my head I saw him, big as life, the pileated woodpecker. He was magnificent, his red head standing out against the green leaves and brown trunk of the tree like a fire engine among unmarked cars. The woodpecker gave a few quick taps on the side of the tree and then flew off, disappearing fast into the woods.

I think I'd been holding my breath the whole time I looked at that bird, so I just sat there, for a moment, breathing hard. I wanted to shout my happiness as I climbed down that tree. I'd forgotten to be scared that I might fall. I'd forgotten about the Scouts and their kindling. I'd seen the woodpecker! When I got to the lowest branch, I swung down to the ground and started running toward the trail. Then I remembered my pack.

I knew that strays were strictly forbidden to disturb the scouting activities, but I wouldn't disturb them much. I'd just ask for my pack and leave. I walked, sort of noisily so I wouldn't catch them off guard, into the clearing.

"Hey," Hans said, smiling his crooked smile at me. "If it isn't Dr. Fenwick."

For a minute I thought he had me confused with my father. Then I remembered the trash scene at the Health Lodge.

"Of the Night Cleanup Patrol," I said back. "Listen, I thought Boy Scouts were supposed to be honest and trustworthy."

"Absolutely," said Hans.

"Then why'd Sinker and Rusty steal my backpack?" I asked, grinning at Sinker.

"Steal it?" Sinker pretended to be shocked. "This is the reward we get for trying to do a good deed and bring you your backpack, which you carelessly left lying under a tree?" He tossed me the pack and I surprised myself by catching it.

Hans was looking at me again in that funny way he had. I wished he'd cut it out.

"What are you doing around here, anyway?" he asked.

Sinker put his hands up to his eyes like binoculars. "Watching the little birdies?" he suggested.

Rusty picked up his Ninja sword and sketched a fast Road Runner in the dirt. "Beep beep!" he said.

Hans pointed to my little green life list book, which was sticking out of a pouch in my pack. "You're a birder?"

Am I Lila Fenwick, Birding Ace? I wondered. And even if I am, do I admit it to T.K.O. Hans? What if he laughs at me for being a bird nerd? Then I remembered how I'd gotten into this spot in the first place, following the *wuck-a-wuck-a-wuck-a*'s, and I remembered how exciting it had been to see that woodpecker. I guessed I'd better confess. I was a birder.

"Yes," I told him. "I'm just beginning though."

Hans reached for my birding book and looked intently at my lists. "This isn't bad for a few days," he said.

"Do . . . you know birds?" I asked.

He nodded. "Bird study was one of my first badges."

"I just saw a pileated woodpecker!" I told him.

"Just two minutes ago. Right in that tree." I pointed to where I'd been perched.

"Hey, that's great!" Hans seemed genuinely excited. He looked up. "They're pretty big, but they're hard to spot." He handed back my little green book. "Congratulations!"

"He was amazing," I began, "with this bright red—"

"Food's ready," Sinker interrupted.

Hans and Troop 97 invited me to stay and have lunch with them, but when I learned that lunch was going to be sauerkraut-and-wiener casserole prepared by Rusty and Sinker for their cooking merit badges, I said no thanks.

I saw a pile of three speckled rocks marking the beginning of the trail from the clearing and headed that way.

"See you!" I said, waving.

"Not if we see you first!" Sinker called.

When I was a little way from the clearing, I stopped, propped my leg up on a rock, opened my birding book, and wrote in big letters: PILEATED WOODPECKER.

Then I began walking in the direction of the Dining Hall, singing to myself as I went: *Wuck-a-wuck-a-wuck-a.*

HOW TO
BE A BUDDY

I was sitting on my bunk, looking at a picture of two red-tailed hawks and wondering if the male and female of the species look exactly alike, how the birds can tell the difference, when I heard Kari's voice.

"You are an *idiot!* A total *jerk!*"

What was she yelling about?

"How was I supposed to know?" came Rita's voice, just as loud and just as angry.

"It doesn't take too much brainpower to figure out you don't ride a horse through an archery range!" Kari shouted. "I just can't believe you!"

Kari stomped up the steps to the Health Lodge, yanked open the screen door, and burst onto the porch.

"Hey!" I said. "What's the problem?"

"She's the problem!" Kari whirled around and stabbed a finger at Rita, who had followed her through the door. "She got Ginger shot!"

"Shot!" I stared at Rita.

Rita was fuming. "I didn't do it on purpose!"

Kari glared at Rita as she talked to me. "Some stupid jerk of a boy at the archery range waves to her and the next thing I know she's riding over to him—right in front of the targets! And an arrow hit Ginger!"

"Is she . . . alive?" I asked.

"Oh, of course she's alive!" Now Kari sounded angry at me.

"Listen!" exclaimed Rita. "I was lucky not to get thrown!"

"I guess you were!" said Kari. "It was so stupid!"

"What happened," I asked, "after she got hit?"

"Ginger bolted for the stable." Kari was striding from one side of the porch to the other as she spoke. "She got there okay and Charlie calmed her down and cleaned out her wound. He said she'd be okay in a day or two, but Charlie was really mad—at her," she pointed again at Rita, "and at me for letting it happen. He says I can't ride Rocky for a week!"

Tears rolled down Kari's face now. She swiped at them with the back of her hand, leaving a dirty brown smear across one cheek. "Those horses are Charlie's babies. If one of 'em's ever sick or something, he stays up with it the whole night."

Kari turned back to Rita. She was so mad she was shaking. "I hate you!" she cried. "You've ruined everything!" With that Kari ran to her room, slamming the door behind her so hard that the Health Lodge shook.

Rita just stood there, fists clenched by her sides. Then she let out a long breath and looked over at me. "I swear," she said. "It was an accident!"

During lunch Kari's seat was empty. I knew where she'd gone—to the stables to check on the horses.

I looked across the table at Rita spreading a mixture of peanut butter and honey onto a slice of bread. I wondered if the peanut butter would go straight to her thighs, like her mother had said. I wondered if Rita should just spread the peanut butter directly onto her upper legs.

Rita looked over at me and said brightly, "I guess it's you and me now."

"Guess so," I said. While I was glad enough to have Rita to hang around with, I felt bad about Kari. Ginger getting shot hadn't been her fault at all. And what would she do all day if she couldn't ride? I'd overheard Mrs. Lindquist telling my mom that since Big Joe died, the only thing that made Kari happy was riding.

"So what do you want to do?" asked Rita.

I thought about it. "My knees should be okay by now. Want to go swimming this afternoon?"

"Uh," said Rita. "Not really."

"How about checking out the Nature Center?" I suggested. "I heard they have some baby rabbits there."

Rita just kept chewing on her honey-peanut butter combo.

I was sure, if I kept thinking, I could find something that the two of us would have fun doing together. But it didn't seem fair that now Rita and I would be big buddies and Kari would be left out in the cold. I hadn't liked it when I'd been left out. Maybe I could come up with a Great Idea for something that we could do together. All three.

We ate in silence, my mental wheels turning the entire time, until my mom said, "I was thinking of doing a little birding down by the base of Eagle Peak. You girls want to come along?"

"Eagle Peak!" I nearly shouted as a Great Idea swooped down and grabbed me. "That's it!"

"It is?" My mom looked puzzled. "Does that mean you want to come?"

"No! I mean, yes!" I tried to explain. "But not this afternoon."

"Sounds very mysterious." My mom got up from the table. "I'll see you all at dinner," she said.

After lunch I volunteered Rita and myself to clear the table. When we had finished, we went into the kitchen and asked the cooks if we could have a bunch of carrots with the tops still on as a get well present for Ginger. Then, carrots in hand, we headed down Red Rock Trail to the stables.

On the way, I tried out my Great Idea on Rita.

"What we should do," I told her, "is go camping on Eagle Peak."

"You mean camp out?" asked Rita. "Like sleep out in the woods?"

"We could sleep in a tent," I said, wondering if that would count as sleeping under the stars on Eagle Peak.

"Just us?" asked Rita. "Me and you?"

"And Kari," I said. "The three of us."

"But what about wild animals? Poisonous snakes, or grizzly bears?"

"Rita," I said, "we might see a raccoon or a possum, or even a deer, but there's about as much chance of finding grizzly bears on Eagle Peak as there is of finding sharks in Lake Coleman."

"Sharks?" said Rita.

"Rita! What do you think the Scouts do around here? They camp out all the time! You think they'd do it if they got mauled by bears?"

But Rita wasn't thinking about bears anymore. "The Scouts camp out? You mean like near where we'd be camping out?"

"They all go to Eagle Peak. It's part of coming to Ironvale. Remember the legend?" I asked Rita. "I'll bet you the place'll be swarming with Scouts."

"Okay, okay, Lila," said Rita as we arrived at the stables. "I'll go on your camping trip."

The stables weren't anything too fancy, just a wooden building smelling of hay and horse manure.

Outside, half a dozen horses with riders on their backs were going around a ring. Two of the Scouts were holding onto the saddle horn instead of the reins, which even *I* knew you weren't supposed to do.

Kari was standing on the fence watching the riding lesson when we got there. She didn't look in our direction. Even though I didn't want to get too close to all those fleabag horses, I wasn't going to let them scare me into giving up my plan. I stepped up on the fence beside Kari. A grizzled man in a western shirt and jeans that bagged in the seat stood in the center of the ring. His wrinkled face was half hidden by a cowboy hat, and he spoke gently to the riders.

"Atta boy," he said to one Scout who looked scared to death to be on a horse. "You're doing just fine. Show ol' Molly who's the boss now. Take up those reins. That's right. You're doing just fine."

The sound of his voice was so comforting that somehow the boy took the reins and seemed to sit up straighter in the saddle.

"That's Charlie?" I asked Kari.

She nodded.

"Is one of these horses Rocky?"

"That one." She pointed to a tall shiny brown horse with a red-brown mane and tail.

Rocky walked slowly around the ring. When he passed the place where Kari was standing on the fence, he shook his head and gave her a little whinny.

"You're my boy!" Kari called to him tenderly, her

anger banished for the moment in the presence of her horse.

When all the riders were going around the ring smoothly, Charlie came over to where we were standing. He pushed his hat back on his head and looked at me.

"You must be Lila," he said. "Your buddies told me that I'd never see you down here at the stables."

I held out my hand. "Hi, Charlie."

His hand felt warm as I shook it.

"You're just in time for a riding class," he said, jerking a thumb over his shoulder at the circling horses. "I can saddle up Lightning in a jiffy."

"No thanks!" I told him. "I'm just looking."

Charlie smiled, and then he looked over at Rita. Her ponytail was drooping on the back of her head like the wilting green ends of the carrots in her hand. "How's Ginger?" she asked in a wavery voice.

"Ginger's okay," he said. "Nothing but a little skin scraped off her flank. But it could have been pretty serious." He shook his head. "Pretty serious."

Rita held the carrots up. "We brought these for Ginger."

Charlie's wrinkled brow relaxed as he took the carrots from Rita. "I'll be sure to tell her where they came from," he said.

Charlie turned to Kari. "You two shouldn't have been riding anywhere near that archery range," he told her.

"I know it." Kari scowled.

"So what I said still goes," Charlie continued. "No riding for three days."

Kari looked confused. "But I thought you said a we . . ."

"Three days," Charlie interrupted. "We'll count today as day one."

He was a softie, Charlie was.

Kari smiled weakly. "Thanks, Charlie," she said. "Thanks a lot."

"Now go on, the three of you!" Charlie shooed us away from the riding ring as if we were pesky horseflies. "No good mooning over it. What's done is done." Charlie looked my way again. "Lila, you keep Kari away from here for a couple of days, okay?"

"Okay!" I called to Charlie. "I've got the perfect way to do it!"

Walking back up Red Rock to Main Camp, Kari was feeling pretty happy because of Charlie's change of heart. So when I told her my idea for a camp out, she was all in favor.

"Might as well," she said. "It'll make the time go faster. Only one thing." Kari stopped walking and turned to face Rita in the trail. "Just don't you talk to me about what happened this morning, okay? Nothing! 'Cause you don't want to remind me how mad I am at you. Got it?"

"Don't worry," said Rita. "I got it."

"It'll be great!" I said in a cheerful voice that sounded a lot like my mother's. "We can pack up today and leave at dawn tomorrow."

We got up in the pitch dark, but by the time we were dressed and ready to go, a pink light glowed in the east from beyond the treetops. We stood outside the Health Lodge, double-checking to make sure we had everything we'd need for our overnight.

I looked behind me at Kari, in her usual jeans and flannel shirt, and at Rita in her usual pink short shorts and her thin purple windbreaker. She was shivering in the morning chill. Both of them had on backpacks with sleeping bags rolled and tied at the bottom.

When we had started planning our trip the day before, and Rita had finally understood that she was going to have to carry all her own camping equipment on her back, she quickly abandoned the Samsonite philosophy of packing and came around to my dad's methods. He had been honored when she'd asked him to help her organize her clothes, mess kit, and wash kit, and he told all of us that Rita had shown a genius for packing light.

Behind Rita stood my mother, who had said a firm *no* to the idea of the three of us camping by ourselves but had promised to keep out of our way. She was wearing her usual sweat suit and the biggest backpack I'd ever seen. She was so proud of her pumping iron muscles that she'd actually volunteered to carry most of the food and cooking equipment, plus the first aid kit and tent! Beneath her sleeping bag roll dangled two shiny saucepans.

"Off you go!" said Mrs. Lindquist, standing next to my father on the steps of the Health Lodge. "Have a wonderful time!"

"Remember," my father called to us, "leaves of three . . . "

"Let it be!" we chorused back to him, and with those words of Great Advice ringing in our ears, we walked off toward Eagle Peak.

The fresh air woke me up as I walked. Soon I was enjoying tramping along a part of Red Rock Trail I'd never been on before. It wove in and out of the woods beside Lake Coleman. *Tchew! Tchew!* I heard the faint call of the ruby-throated hummingbird. *Chick-a-dee-dee-dee!* Chickadees, I thought. *TUM TUM TUM DE DUM!* I wondered if there were a trumpeter swan overhead, until I recognized the sound of the distant reveille bugle. I smiled, thinking that at least this morning it couldn't wake me up.

After about ten minutes on the trail, a new sound met my ears. It was my stomach growling.

"Anybody else hungry?" I asked.

"I'm starving!" said Kari. "When were we planning to stop and eat?"

"Not for half an hour," said Rita, who had been in charge of making our camping plan. "But I'm so hungry I could eat a horse!"

"*What* did you say?" asked Kari in a threatening tone.

"Horrors!" I blurted quickly before Kari could start thinking about Rita and horses. "She said, 'I'm so hungry! Horrors!' Right, Rita? And I'm hungry too." I turned to my mom. "Can't we stop sooner?"

"Hmmm," said my mom. "There is a cooking site not too far from here. If no one's using it, I guess we could."

"Onward to breakfast!" I called, and we kept hiking.

A few minutes later we reached a small clearing. Thick spiky bushes that reminded me of Kari's hairdo surrounded it and in the center was a big stone fireplace with a chimney. Just the other side of the clearing, we could see the lake.

"Now," said my mom, squatting down to unbuckle her pack, "I'll be breakfast cook."

I hoped she wouldn't try any of her health food recipes.

"You girls can be in charge of lunch and supper. Hey—listen!" she said, as she tossed each of us a giant orange to start off our meal. "If you're really quiet, you can hear the boys—all the way back at camp."

"Who cares about boys?" said Kari, stabbing her thumb into her orange and ripping down the peel. "All I care about is food!"

The oranges were so sweet—and juicy. By the time we polished off two each, we all had orange juice dripping from our elbows.

"Help!" Rita cried, holding her sticky arms away from her body.

Then Kari stood up. "I'm going to rinse my hands off in the lake."

"Me too," said Rita.

"Me three," I said.

Rita led the way to the lake. We were just a clump of bushes away from it when suddenly Rita froze in her tracks and gasped.

"What's wrong?" I asked.

Rita turned to us, a startled look on her face. She was pointing to the lake. "Th-there!" she stammered.

Quickly Rita stooped down, facing away from the lake, as if hiding. Kari and I hunkered down beside her.

"What's in the lake?" whispered Kari.

"Boys!" Rita whispered back.

"We're hiding from boys?" I asked.

Rita nodded. "They're swimming!"

"Swimming?" Kari looked puzzled.

"And they're not wearing any suits!" whispered Rita.

"Rita!" Kari broke into a pointy smile. "It's the Polar Bear club! They come over to this part of the lake every morning for a dip!"

"They could at least wear suits!" huffed Rita.

"Now we know why they call it polar *bare!*" I joked.

"It's no big deal," Kari said. Obviously having brothers took away the shock value of suitless Boy Scouts.

"But what if they see us?" objected Rita. "They'll think we're here on purpose! To spy on them!"

Kari got a funny look in her eyes. "Well, as long as we're here . . . " she said, and she peeked through the bushes.

I knelt beside Kari and took a peek myself. Rita must have some great eyesight! I thought. All I could see was a lot of churning splashing water.

"I can't really see much," I said, turning around.

"Me neither," said Kari softly, not moving from her spot behind the bushes. "But I can fix that."

"Kari!" Rita screeched in a whisper. "Whatever you're going to do . . . *don't!*"

But Kari just glanced at Rita, still with that funny look on her face. Then she turned toward the lake, spit her retainer out into her hand, and took a deep breath. She bared her teeth, closed her eyes, and gave out with the loudest, shrillest whistle I've ever heard. It sounded exactly like Coach's whistle back at N.A.P.!

Rita and I just stared as Kari fell at our feet, laughing like crazy.

"What did you do?" I asked.

"Take a look!" said Kari. "Go on!" She was pointing toward the lake, where suddenly the splashing had stopped.

I peered through the branches again. The Polar Bears were standing up, wading through the water.

They seemed to be grouping themselves in pairs, grabbing hold of a hand of a nearby Polar Bear and holding their clasped hands high above their heads.

"It's Buddy Check!" cackled Kari as she raised herself up to her knees to watch the Boy Scouts of America standing like twin statues in the lake. "No one's ever allowed to go swimming without a buddy, a partner. For safety, you know." She parted the branches of her bush to get a better view.

The Polar Bears seemed to be looking around, wondering who'd blown the whistle.

"How long will they stand like that?" I whispered to Kari.

"They're waiting for the signal to end Buddy Check," she said.

"Give the signal!" begged Rita. "Before they look over here and see us!"

With that Kari repeated her powerful whistle, and the Polar Bears plunged back in for their icy morning dip.

The three of us crawled, semi-G.I. Joe style, out of the brush until we were a safe distance from the lake.

"Anybody get a good look?" asked Kari as we stood up and brushed ourselves off. Our sticky orange-juicy hands and arms were coated with dirt.

"Well, I think I saw something," I said. "But the water was a little deep for—you know."

"Yeah," said Kari. "Oh, well. At least we tried. How about you, Rita? You see anything?"

"I didn't look," said Rita primly, and then she

walked stiffly ahead of us until we were back at the cooking site.

My mom was humming to herself as she stuck a stiff blade of grass into the center of one of the muffins she was baking to see if it was done. She looked up and gasped as we appeared, smeared with a red-orange coating of Ironvale dust. We rinsed off with our drinking water, and Kari and I told my mom about our encounter with the Polar Bear Club. She tried not to laugh, but she couldn't help herself, especially when Kari and I held our hands up to show her the Buddy Check position.

My mom shook her head. "You girls!" she said, giving each of us a warm banana muffin on a little aluminum plate. "What have I let myself in for, volunteering to be your chaperon in these wild woods?" Then I guess she must have noticed that Rita was being awfully quiet. "Something the matter, Rita?" she asked.

"We were lucky they didn't see us," Rita said hotly. "But it's their fault anyway, swimming without suits."

"Haven't you ever been skinny-dipping?" asked my mom.

"Been what?" asked Rita.

"Skinny-dipping," said my mom. "Swimming naked."

"No," said Rita. "Why would I want to do that?"

"You'll just have to try it some time," said my mom. "Then you'll see. Listen, don't feel bad about catching the Polar Bears off guard—you didn't do it on purpose."

But Rita looked at my mother as if she were indecent, while I wondered why Rita was suddenly such a prude. At N.A.P. she paraded around in her purple bikini, which was about ten square inches of material away from not wearing anything.

When we'd each finished two big muffins (they were the normal kind, thank goodness, with no wheat germ thrown in) with a side of watercress, we cleaned up the cooking site the Boy Scout way, leaving no sign that we'd ever been there. Then, packs on our backs, we hit the trail.

We walked quite a while in a comfortable silence. I kept my eyes alert for flashes of color that might be birds as my ears filled with chirps and twitters. Even my nose seemed to be enjoying this hike, with the mixed smells of pine needles, wild flowers, and good old plain fresh air. After a bit we came to a fork in the trail marked with rocks painted blue. I'd never seen a trail marked with painted rocks before—let alone blue. My mom, in the lead, hesitated and then she looked back at Kari. "You know where Blue Rock Trail leads, don't you?"

"Sure!" Kari said. "Stray Creek. Hey! Are you thinking what I think you're thinking?"

My mom nodded.

"Whoopie!" shouted Kari. "I haven't been there yet this summer!"

And with that Kari and my mom took off running down Blue Rock Trail, leaving Rita and me to follow along as best we could. In a few minutes we came alongside a creek. For a while it was only a few inches deep, but beside a rocky bluff it widened and deepened into a sparkling clear pool.

"Last one in's a rotten egg," said my mother, unshouldering her pack and kicking off her shoes.

Kari was out of her jeans and shirt like lightning and with a giant splash she dove into the creek, but my mom had beat her to it.

I watched them for a moment, swimming and diving like seals.

"I'm coming in!" I called to my mom. "Knees or no knees."

"It's been almost two weeks," she called back. "They'll be okay."

Then I, too, peeled off my clothes, shoved my specs into my pack, and raced into the creek. No water had ever felt like that! It was cool, but not cold. Gently the current tickled by me like a liquid breeze. Flipping over I backstroked to the bluff and back again, feeling sure that my time out for injuries hadn't ruined my swimming career. I felt such a part of the water, like a fish, like a dolphin, like I belonged there.

Rita stood stiffly on the rocky beach.

"Come in, Rita!" I called. "You have to try it!"

"This is a boy's camp, right?" she called back. "What if they come here?"

"They can't," shouted my mother. "Blue Rock Trail

is off limits to the boys. It's strictly for female strays. Scout's honor, Rita!"

"That's why it's called Stray Creek!" yelled Kari.

But Rita planted herself firmly on a rock. Without my specs she looked a bit blurry, but she seemed to have her arms folded across her chest and be looking away from us.

My mom swam over to me. "I'm going to talk to Rita for a minute," she said. "You and Kari be buddies, okay?"

"No," I told her, squinting at the pouting Rita. "I'll go. You and Kari be buddies."

Boy, was I sick of this scene. Two together, one left out. I was determined not to have it be this way anymore! And I was going to do something about it too. I just didn't know what.

I swam to the edge of the creek until it was so shallow my stomach scraped the bottom. I pulled myself to my feet and tottered over the rocks to put on my long T-shirt and glasses. Then I went and sat down by Rita.

I didn't know exactly what I was going to say, but I didn't have to worry about it because Rita started in.

"I can't believe this," she said. "Even your *mother!*"

"It's just us and it's just skinny-dipping," I told her. "It doesn't seem that awful."

"But what if someone sees us!" she said.

"Like we saw the Polar Bears?" I asked. "They won't, but even if they did, so what? It's just skin."

Rita sighed. "Well, even if I wanted to swim like that, without a suit, I couldn't."

"Why not?" I asked her.

" 'Cause I can't swim *with* a suit. I don't know how."

This caught me by surprise. "But this summer, you were at the pool," I began.

"*At* the pool," she said, "but not *in* the pool. I'm sort of . . . scared of deep water."

I looked at my mom and Kari happily floating and flipping in the creek. Water had always been more a home to me than land. It seemed too bad that Rita should miss out on how good the water could feel. Maybe now it was my turn to let Rita in on some of the S.O.S.—the Secrets of Swimming!

"Well," I told her, "you just have to show the water who's boss."

Rita frowned. "What?"

"That's what you told me," I said, "when you wanted me to get on a horse."

"But that's different!" Rita said.

"It's different," I admitted, "but not that different. I'm scared of horses just like you're scared of the water."

A brain wave crashed inside my head. Before I had a chance to think about the Great Idea that was washing up on the shores of my mind, I was offering it to Rita.

"I'll make you a deal. I'll probably regret it for the rest of my life, but here goes. If you'll give Stray

Creek a try, I'll . . . I'll try riding Lightning."

Rita was suspicious at first. "You want me to try swimming so much that you'll get on a horse?"

What had I done? I clenched my teeth and nodded yes.

Rita looked almost thoughtful for a moment. Then she started firing questions at me as if she were a lawyer.

"I just have to get in the water. That's it?"

"And stay for ten minutes," I said.

"Then you'll ride Lightning for ten minutes?"

"Stay in for five minutes," I said.

"How deep do I have to go?"

"Up to your neck."

"Waist," Rita said.

"How about armpits?"

"Okay. Five minutes up to the armpits. That's the total deal?"

We shook on it.

Then Rita drew a deep breath. "Actually," she said, "I am sweating hot." She rummaged through her pack. "I stuck in my bikini. You know, for sunbath ing." She gave me a big smile and said, "You didn't make skinny-swimming part of the deal."

"Rita!" I shouted.

But she just ignored me as she pulled out her suit and went behind a tree to change into it. I guessed that while Rita didn't object to showing *almost* all of her body, she must just be shy about parts of it. Come to think of it, I'd never seen her totally undressed the whole time we were at Ironvale. She always went into the bathroom to change. But then there was short little Kari, with bigger breasts than my mom's (not that that was saying very much) skinny-dipping away without an ounce of shyness. I wondered if I'd feel like Kari or like Rita or like something in between if I ever got rid of my third grade shape.

I shed my T-shirt and dove back into the creek. I was already swimming when I heard Rita squeal, "Yikes!" as she dipped her pearl pink piggies into the water.

"Your five minutes won't start until you're up to your armpits," I informed Rita.

"What are you guys yelling about?" called Kari.

"Lila made a deal!" Rita shouted back as she took another teensy step into the creek. "She said she'd ride Lightning if I'd get in the water."

I swam to where Rita was standing, and Kari met us in one porpoise dive. "You're going to love Lightning, Lila!" she shouted. "This is a great deal!"

After Rita got used to the water temperature, she let Kari and me show her how to put her face in the water and blow bubbles, the first step in learning to swim. I had to hand it to Rita. She was giving it her all.

After a while my mom said she'd had enough swimming. "Can the three of you be buddies if I get out?" she asked.

Without even thinking about it I grabbed Rita's hand and Kari's hand, raising them high in the Buddy Check pose.

"I wish I had a camera," my mom said, looking back at us as she kicked toward shore, "to take a picture of you bathing beauty buddies."

"Bare beauty buddies!" I yelled, jumping up and plunging back into the creek with an enormous splash.

"Body beauty buddies!" shouted Kari, bounding out of the water the way I had done and falling back with a giant ker-plop.

Rita just stared.

"Belly boodie buddies!" I shouted, making an even bigger leap and lunge.

"Boom-boom buddies!" yelled Kari. *Splash!*

"Boola-boola buddies!" I cried. *Ker-splash!*

And then, over the sloshing creek water and over our hoots of laughter, came the voice of Rita Morgan, loud and clear.

"Bosom buddy buddies!" she called. Then she held her nose, gave a little jump, and plopped under water, ponytail and all. Up she came, grinning and gasping for breath, and I saw that Kelly and Gayle had been right about Rita's bikini that day back at N.A.P. It had come off.

I grabbed the tiny purple top as it floated by me on the current, and then we all collapsed in a splashy heap, laughing like crazy. All three of us.

HOW TO
BE PREPARED

Be prepared. That's the Boy Scout motto. When I'd thought up the idea for the Eagle Peak camping trip, I was prepared to sleep out under the stars, to do a little hiking, a little cooking over a fire, and a little birding to add an owl or two to my life list.

But I wasn't prepared for the peak's eagle to be completely hidden by the cumulonimbus clouds that began to gather the minute we reached our campsite nor for the steady sheets of rain that fell all night long.

We bunched together for warmth in our little tent. Since it was too wet to make a fire, we dined on bread and butter, carrot sticks, dried apricots, and the apples we'd brought along to bake Apple Betty. We washed it all down with bug juice.

"I guess if we can't see any stars on Eagle Peak it won't exactly count as 'sleeping under the stars,' " I said.

"The stars are still there," said my mom.

I shook my head. "I don't know. I have a feeling we're not going to find out any big secrets."

"The big secret is this weather!" exclaimed Rita. "Didn't you check the weather report, Lila?"

"What are you," I asked, "a fair-weather camper?"

"Yes!" cried Rita, Kari, and my mom together.

"Me too," I admitted, looking out the tent flap at the flood and the mud and feeling responsible for everyone's misery. "But," I added cheerily, "at least we're dry and comfortable in here."

"Dry?" said Rita. "I'm mildewing!"

"Think of it as a giant humidifier," I told her. "Anyway, things could always be worse." And little did I know that before long, they would be.

When I opened my eyes the next morning and peered out the tent flap, the sky was the kind of clean brilliant blue that comes only after a hard rain. A light mist hovered among the cedars, and just a few puddles dotted our campsite, which, amazingly enough, looked nearly as dusty as it had before the downpour. And there, right above me, were the huge boulders that formed an eagle's head. They looked less like an eagle this close. Still, I'd done it. I'd camped out at Eagle Peak just as I had promised myself I would when I was up a tree.

I lay in my sleeping bag for a minute, trying to figure out if I felt different. Had I learned anything that I hadn't known before? Disappointed, I realized that the only thing I knew for sure was that when one drinks several cups of bug juice before going to bed, one must make an early morning trip to the woods. I wriggled out of my sleeping bag quietly, trying not to wake anyone, crawled outside in my long T-shirt, which had doubled as a nightgown, and went behind a clump of birches.

I shivered in the cool morning air and hurried back to the tent, reaching in to pull out my jeans, a sweat shirt, and sneakers. Then I went on a kindling-gathering mission, and by the time my mom, Kari, and Rita woke up I had a nice little fire going and was stirring up some pancake batter.

I only scorched the first batch. The rest were definitely above House of Pancakes quality. We all sat around the fire eating them as fast as we could, making up for last night's cold supper.

When we finished, my mom went back into the tent and came out with two little packages strangely wrapped in big oak leaves and tied with chains of clover.

"This was the best wrapping job I could do in the wilderness," she said as she handed one leafy present to Rita and one to Kari.

For a minute I felt left out, until I saw what was inside: official Boy Scout birding books that I'd seen at the Ironvale store. My mom had crossed out Boy

Scout and penned in a new title that read: The Official Buddies Birding Book!

"I thought you two might want to start life lists," she told them, "the way Lila and I have been doing. We could take a little birding hike this morning."

"Thanks, Mrs. Fenwick," said Rita, flipping rapidly through the lined pages of the book. "How many birds do I have to see before I catch up with you, Lila?"

"I've got twenty-nine species," I told her.

"So I'd need thirty," Rita muttered.

"Thank you," said Kari, tracing over the letters in her book's title. Then she added in a quiet voice, "My dad used to be a big birder."

"Who do you think got me started on birding?" my mom said.

"My dad?" Kari asked.

My mom nodded. "The first year I came to Ironvale to visit Phil, your mom and dad had just gotten married and were running the Health Lodge. Your dad used to drag us all out of bed before reveille and have us on the trails by dawn looking for birds." My mom smiled, remembering. "He was the obsessed kind of birder who'd go to any length to see a new species."

"Like what?" asked Kari.

"Well, if there were birds he knew were native to this part of the country and he hadn't seen them, he'd learn their songs," my mom said. "He had this set of tapes. He said he'd practice learning the songs all winter."

"I know those tapes." Kari smiled. Then she grew solemn again. "I just never paid much attention to them."

My mom reached over and gave Kari's shoulder a little rub. "Then," she went on, "come summer, in the early morning, Big Joe would go out and settle himself in the woods and start calling the birds. And sooner or later—sometimes it took weeks—but he'd always get those birds to come and see who was calling them!"

"Wait a minute," said Rita. "Isn't that cheating? To call the birds like that?"

"Not at all," said my mom. "It's just that very few people are willing to go to all the trouble of learning the birdcalls."

My mom smiled at Kari. "Big Joe got me started on birding and now I'm going to get *you* hooked. Fair?"

Kari didn't look up. She just nodded her head. I couldn't exactly tell, but I thought she might have tears in her eyes. This time, though, they weren't angry ones.

"You know," I said to break the silence, "Hans Pearson is a birder."

"Hans?" chirped Rita. "Really?"

And so it was that my mother's plans for a morning of birding met with everyone's approval.

We all changed into shorts then, since the day promised to be a hot one. Then we washed the dishes, packed up our tent and sleeping bags and left them stacked at the side of the campsite. We stuck a few light things—our birding books, binoculars, and extra T-shirts—in our backpacks. My mom tucked sandwiches and little cans of pineapple juice in hers. She'd kept the juice icy cold all night by putting the cans in a string bag and dangling them in the stream, anchored by a rock. We were prepared to eat lunch on the trail and come back later in the afternoon to pick up the rest of our gear before heading back to Main Camp.

Black Rock Trail led down from our campsite, away from Eagle Peak. We followed it. It took us through the woods and then ran parallel to a big field of wild flowers. In the field Rita and Kari began birding with a bang as my mom identified two common nighthawks circling in broad daylight. Then they got the usual sparrow-cardinal-blue jay starters. Rita was thrilled to be able to count seven birds in half an hour.

"At this rate I'll have thirty types before lunch!" she crowed, sending a pair of does that had been standing still as lawn ornaments bounding off into the woods.

"Are *you* dears ready for a birding break?" asked my mom.

"I am," declared Rita. "I haven't seen a new bird in ten minutes!"

We dropped our packs on a big flat rock and scampered to the middle of the field, settling down in a dewy clover patch. My mom showed us how to make clover chains, the way she had done to wrap the birding books. A clover stem is tough, and you can make a little loop knot in it and stick in the stem of another clover, then pull the loop tight just under the flower. If you keep doing this, over and over, you get a long chain of clovers.

While we made clover necklaces, bracelets, and crowns, my mom did a series of leg-stretching exercises followed by a deep breathing routine. "So!" she said peppily. "Who's ready to get going again?"

The three of us were silent.

"We're burned-out, Mrs. Fenwick," said Rita at last.

"Birding burnout," my mom repeated. "Okay. I'd say you did very nicely for your first time out."

"Why don't you go ahead?" I asked my mom, as I waved a bee away from my clover crown. "We'll hang around here, and you can come back and get us when you're burned-out."

My mom looked thoughtful. "Well, I think I've heard the call of a loggerhead shrike. . . . "

"Not the *shrike?*" asked Kari, sending us all into a fit of birding giggles.

"Yes," my mom said, trying to remain serious, "the shrike, and I wouldn't mind just going to the top of this ridge for a while to see if I could spot him."

"By all means, go get him!" Rita said.

"You've talked me into it," said my mom. "I won't

be long. Just stay in this field, okay?"

We promised—and this time I planned to keep my promise and stay out of trouble—and my mom took off to find her shrike.

"Just remember," I called after her, "three shrikes and you're out!"

For a while we lolled in the grass, picking clover, working mindlessly on a clover chain jump rope and talking.

"So which Scout do you think is absolutely the cutest?" Rita asked us.

Kari and I looked at each other.

"Shep Dorty," Kari said.

"Come on!" Rita insisted. "For serious!"

"Which one do you think is?" I asked Rita.

"No contest," she replied. "Hans is definitely number one. But Stinker is cute too."

"Sinker," I corrected her.

"What do you think about Rusty?" Rita asked.

I shrugged. "He's a good drawer."

"That's *not* what I meant!" Rita said.

"Let's try the jump rope," said Kari.

I scrambled up to take an end, glad that I hadn't had to say that I, too, thought Hans was number one.

Rita and I tried to turn the chain so Kari could jump, but after one turn it broke into three pieces, which we added to our jewelry.

Rita began turning cartwheels in the clover then,

while I leaped after her, happy not to be bumping into anything. I watched Kari, thinking that she was about to turn a cartwheel, too, but she did a handstand and began walking on her hands. She made it look as easy as walking on feet. Then, as gracefully as she had gone up, she let her feet tilt backward toward the ground until she was doing a back bend, from which she straightened to a stand. Her normally pale face was red from being upside down.

"That was great!" I told her.

"Think you could show me how to do a handstand?" asked Rita. "And walk like that?"

I wondered if Rita would ka-boom walking on her hands.

Kari grinned. "It's easy. You just have to keep your weight balanced directly over your hands while you walk."

"Easy for you maybe," I said. "I have trouble keeping my weight balanced directly over my *feet* when I walk!"

Kari laughed, then held her hands up and lightly planted them on the ground as she swung her feet up in the air. Again she began walking on her hands through the clover.

But this time, after a few steps, she gave a little yelp and tumbled to the ground. At first I thought it was part of some fancy trick of hers, but somehow the fall looked too awkward.

"Kari?" I asked. "You okay?"

She didn't answer. Rita and I ran up to where she was sitting on the ground. I saw again that angry look on her face, the look I'd seen when I first shone my flashlight on her by the trash can. She was holding tightly to her hand.

"What happened?" asked Rita.

"I . . . I'm not sure," said Kari, scowling down at her palm. "There was something in the grass . . . something sharp."

"Like broken glass?" I asked her.

Kari shrugged.

"Is it bleeding?" asked Rita.

Kari shook her head.

"Let me look," I said.

Kari held out her hand. I saw a small red spot.

"I see something," I told her. "A splinter or a bite maybe."

Kari pulled her hand away. "It's no big deal," she said. She started to get up but staggered and fell back down on the clover. "I feel sort of dizzy," she said.

"Just sit there," I told her. "Don't get up until you feel okay." I hoped I was saying the right thing. I wished my mom would get back.

I didn't know what to do, but I felt that I had to do something.

"Maybe Rita and I can look in the grass and find whatever it was that stuck you," I said.

"We'll find it, for sure!" said Rita, trying to sound confident.

We got down on our hands and knees and began raking our fingers through all the patches that had been crushed by Kari's hands. It seemed a hopeless thing to do, but to my surprise I spotted a small bee lying smashed and dead in the clover.

"Hey!" I said, picking up the bee and holding it for Kari to see. "Look what I found!"

But Kari didn't look. Rita and I had been so busy searching in the clover that we hadn't paid any attention to her for a few minutes. Now her eyes were shut and she was curled up into a ball, breathing hard, with a wheezing sound. Her hand was really swelling.

"You . . . you think you can walk, Kari?" I asked. But she just moaned. She didn't even seem to hear me.

"I wish your mom would get back!" Rita whined, looking frightened.

"I think Kari's allergic to bee stings," I said, more to myself than to Rita. "I've heard of that."

I knelt close beside Kari. Her hand seemed to be getting bigger all the time. Then, with a whimper, she slumped over.

"Kari?" I said. "Kari?" I looked up. "Rita, Kari doesn't even know we're talking to her!"

Rita looked very scared. "What do we do?" she whimpered. She was starting to cry.

I tried to think fast. *What do we do?* I was scared too. *What do we do?*

I looked down at Kari again, and my heart nearly

stopped. Her skin was red and blotchy. And I couldn't see her breathing!

"Kari!" I shouted. She didn't answer. Then she took an odd, shaky breath.

Breathing that started and stopped. Mottled color. In the back of my mind something was coming into focus. Apathy. Kari certainly didn't care what was going on around her. My mother's first aid class! Her test! What else? Pale cold clammy skin. I felt Kari's forehead. The skin was cool and moist, definitely clammy. Kari was in shock!

In my mind I heard my mother's voice in the kitchen at home. *Elevate the legs eight to twelve inches. This helps send blood back toward the heart and keeps it beating.* Then it had been helping my mom study for a little quiz. Now it was the real thing. *People die from shock,* she'd said.

"Rita," I said. "Go get our packs. Hurry!"

Rita raced off and was back in an instant.

"I'm going to pick up Kari's legs. You stick her pack under her feet. Okay?"

Rita nodded.

Gently I raised Kari's feet and propped them up on the pack.

"This is horrible!" cried Rita. She knelt beside me, shaking her hands up and down. "How could a bee sting do this? I can't stand it!"

Bee sting! Maybe there was something for bee stings in the first aid kit! Had my mom thought to pack it? Or was it with our sleeping bags and all the cooking equipment at the campsite? I unzipped my mom's pack and yanked out her jacket. Our sandwiches and the juice cans tumbled onto my lap.

"Yikes! These are cold as ice!" I said, picking up a can. "Ice. I think ice is good for swelling." I looked over at Rita. "Have you ever heard that?"

"I . . . I don't know!" wailed Rita.

"I think so," I muttered. "Try holding this on her hand, where the sting is."

Still sniveling, Rita took the cold can and pressed it against Kari's swollen palm.

As I looked at Kari lying so still in the damp grass, my mother's voice echoed in my head again. *Place a blanket over the victim if he is cold or damp.* We didn't have a blanket. But we had a jacket. Quickly I put my mom's jacket over Kari to keep her from losing body heat.

Now I reached in the pack again, and I found the first aid kit. As soon as I opened it I saw a bright yellow tube with a black insect stamped on it. I picked it up. "For Insect Sting Emergencies," it said. I tore open the paper covering, wondering how I'd be able to get Kari to swallow medicine. But when I saw what was inside the wrapper, I dropped it and jumped back.

"Lila!" cried Rita. "What's wrong?"

"I . . . I found what we need," I told her. "But it's . . . it's . . ." I picked up the tube and read the words from its side. "It says, 'auto-injector'!"

"Injector?" Rita looked horrified. "That's a shot!"

I nodded. The injector looked like a large syringe, but instead of a plunger at one end, it had a gray cap, and instead of a needle at the other end, it had a thick black tip with a red center.

"A shot!" repeated Rita. "How are we supposed to know how to do all of this? Why isn't your mother back?"

Rita had dropped the juice can and was shaking her hands up and down again.

"We can't panic!" I practically shouted. "We'll read the directions and we'll just do what they say!"

"I can't!" wailed Rita.

"Rita!" I tried to make my voice sound commanding. "You have to help!" Help—that's what we needed, and fast! "I think you should go try to find my mom."

"But Lila," she wailed, "what if I *can't* find her?"

"You've got to! Follow the path, the black rocks," I said. "Hurry!"

"Mrs. Fenwick!" Rita yelled as her feet pounded up the trail. "Mrs. Fenwiiiiiiiiick!"

I looked back at Kari and positioned the juice can so it was under her hand. She looked less blotchy, more pale now. I was so scared!

Swallowing hard to keep from crying, I read the directions from the auto-injector. They were plenty clear. Kari needed a shot of this long unpronounceable medicine, and I was going to have to give it to her.

Pull out gray safety cap. I pulled.

Place black tip on outer thigh. I put the tip of the injector against the upper part of Kari's left leg.

Push hard until you hear or feel the injector function. I wondered if I'd be able to tell if it was working. I held my breath and pushed, *hard!* I heard a small click.

Hold in place ten seconds. One one-thousand, two one-thousand, three one-thousand. Was it working? Four one-thousand, five one-thousand. I was counting too fast! Six one-thousand, seven one-thousand. Kari's small. What if this is too much medicine for her? Eight one-thousand, nine one-thousand, ten one-thousand. With trembling hands I pulled up on the injector.

Please let this be right! I chanted.

I watched Kari for a couple of minutes, but she didn't move. I remembered about checking for a pulse in her neck and was feeling around, trying to find it, when Kari let out a soft moan. That moan was the best sound I've ever heard!

Kari opened her eyes. At first she looked confused and then scared. "What's going on?" she asked in a hoarse whisper.

"You got stung by a bee," I told her.

Kari shook her head slightly and closed her eyes again.

It seemed like I sat there, just watching Kari breathe, for a long time. At last I heard my mom and Rita running toward us. It was such a relief when my mom knelt down by Kari that I started crying and laughing at the same time!

When I calmed down I told my mom what had happened and what I'd done. She listened and then gave me a hard hug. "You did exactly right, Lila," she whispered. "I'm so sorry I wasn't here!"

Then out of the first aid kit my mom took a razor blade. She began scraping at Kari's swollen palm. "It was a good idea to put that cold can on her hand," she said softly as she scraped. "It slowed the poison going through her system."

"What are you doing?" sniffed Rita, kneeling nearby.

"Trying to remove the bee's venom sac," my mother said. "There! Got it!"

In a few minutes Kari opened her eyes again. She gave my mom a small smile. "See your shrike?" she whispered.

After Kari had rested for a while Rita and I helped her climb on my muscle mom for a piggyback ride back to camp.

"Giddyup," said Kari weakly.

Rita and I followed with the packs. We stopped by our Eagle Peak campsite to pick up what we could carry, and then we started down the trail back to Main Camp. Luckily most of it was downhill.

An hour later our worn-out little camping party staggered up the steps of the Health Lodge, looking like a much different crew than had left it so cheerily the morning before. My mom took Kari to her bunk and gently put her down. Then she went to tell Mrs. Lindquist what had happened.

Rita and I dropped our loads with a crash on the porch floor and flopped down on our bunks, just catching our breath, not even talking. Walking with the heavy packs plus the Kari scare had made me more tired than I'd ever been before. The next thing I knew, someone was shaking my shoulder.

"Lila!" It was my dad's voice. "Wake up, honey!"

I opened my eyes. "I wasn't sleeping."

"Well, you could have fooled us," he said. "You've been lying here for over four hours!"

"Where's Rita?" I asked sleepily.

"She went on up to the Dining Hall with your mother," he said. "It's nearly supper time."

"Kari!" I sat up suddenly, remembering.

"She's fine, resting in her room. She'll be okay, thanks to some quick thinking. How'd you know to elevate her feet that way? And to keep her warm with a jacket?"

"I helped Mom study for her test, remember?"

"Well, you certainly passed this one!" he said.

"Why did a little bee sting make Kari so sick?" I asked.

"A few—*very* few—people are extremely sensitive to bee venom. It's like poison to them. And they can die from it if it's not treated properly." He looked at me seriously. "Giving Kari that shot of epinephrine probably saved her life."

"Shot of what?" I asked.

"Epi-neff-rin," he said clearly. "It gets the heart pumping and the blood circulating again." He smiled proudly at me and then added, "Why don't you clean up a little bit now and we'll go up to dinner?"

"Can I see Kari first?" I asked my dad.

"Sure," he said. "Just stay for a minute though. She needs her rest."

I knocked on Kari's open door and tiptoed into her room. "Kari?" I whispered.

"Hey," she said from her bed. Her bushy blond head looked so little on the pillow. She held up her hand. Even with a bandage on, it looked more like a normal hand now, not so swollen. "I hear I slept through all the excitement," she said, grinning her pointy grin.

I sat down on the foot of her bed. "You feel okay?"

"Not bad," she said. "A little dizzy. I get room service tonight. My brothers are bringing Mom and me a supper tray from the Dining Hall. Hope it's not mystery meat."

"I know what you mean," I said. "How long do you have to stay in bed?"

"Your dad says I can get up tomorrow," Kari said. "And the next day I can ride Rocky. I just have to carry one of these things with me all the time." She reached over to her bedside table and picked up an auto-injector.

"Good idea!" I told her. "Well, my dad said I had to make this a quick visit."

"Come back after dinner," she said. And as I got to the door of her room she added, "Lila?"

"What?"

"Thanks."

When my dad and I walked into the Dining Hall, Shep Dorty was already giving his evening announcements. He was saying that so far there were twenty-six Scouts still eligible for membership in the Polar Bear Club!

We slipped into our seats at Doc's table. My mom squeezed my hand. Rita gave me a wink. I noticed that her ponytail was riding high this evening and she was dressed in a shiny plum-colored sweater with a scalloped collar that I hadn't seen before. I listened as Shep told about the plans for the evening's campfire. Then he said, "We have a very important award to present at this time."

I hadn't eaten since the pancakes early that morning and I couldn't wait to dig into dinner, even if it was mystery meat. I hoped the presentation would be short.

"Let me introduce the person," said Shep, "who is going to make the presentation. Rita Morgan!"

Rita Morgan?

Rita gave me another little wink and then swiveled out of her place on the bench and ka-boomed steadily up to the platform where Shep was standing. The Ironvale Dining Hall filled with foot stomping, hand clapping, and loud whistles.

Shep lowered his mike for Rita, saying into it as he did so, "All right, Scouts! Let's listen to Rita now."

Rita waited until the last clap sounded and then said, "I am *so* happy to be here tonight . . . "

This simple statement was greeted with another round of applause. Rita rolled her baby blues around and looked at Shep as if to say that she couldn't help it.

What's going on? I wondered. I looked at my dad, but he just grinned.

" . . . to present an award," Rita finally went on. "Since we strays don't get merit badges like you Boy Scouts do, it seems only fair to give a special award to a very special stray! Today, up at Eagle Peak, Kari Lindquist was stung by a bee and had an allergetic . . . allergenic . . . anyway, a *very* serious reaction that could have totally killed her if it had not been for the quick thinking of Lila Fenwick!"

I felt my face get burning hot. The Scouts were cheering and clapping like crazy again.

"Lila!" Rita's voice boomed into the microphone. "Come up and get your award!"

My head was whirling, but at least I still had the sense not to try to ka-boom up to the platform. I was very careful going up the steps to stand beside Rita. I heard her telling the Boy Scouts of America about what had happened up in the clover field that morning and how she had panicked but how I'd kept my head and had known just what to do. I thought she'd never stop, but finally Shep leaned over the mike and said, "Let's show everyone Lila's award."

With that Rita held up a drawing in a rustic twig frame. It was a cartoon showing a girl with long brown hair and glasses with her foot raised on a big bumblebee that had *XX*'s for eyes to show that he was dead. Underneath, it said: "For Lila Fenwick, who really knows how to BEE PREPARED!"

Shep tilted the mike over to me to see if I had anything to say, and I saw a look of gratitude on his face when I limited my remarks to, "Thank you."

There was more clapping and whistling while Rita and I went back to our table. As we walked Rita put her head close to mine. "How do you like it?" she asked. "The award!" she added, when I looked blank.

"Oh, it's great," I told her.

We sat down at Doc's table again, and I passed my award around for everyone to see. When it came back to me, Rita confessed, "Rusty drew it. But it was my idea. And look," Rita pointed to a shape in the background of the picture.

I squinted. "What is it?"

"Eagle Peak!" Rita traced its outline with a freshly polished finger. "You know, the legend! Don't you get it?"

I must have looked blank again, because Rita gave me an exasperated glance and then leaned over and whispered in my ear, "It's the secret! What you discovered about yourself! This is it! I mean, did you ever *think* you could give somebody a shot and save their *life?* You were prepared!"

"I just hope," I told Rita as she passed me a platter of mystery meat, "that I'll never have to be *that* prepared again."

HOW TO DISCOVER
THE SECRETS
OF THE STARS

"You can do it!" Rita pulled the largest of her Samsonites from under her camp bed.

"You can!" echoed Kari, sitting cross-legged on my bunk.

"I don't think so!" I moaned.

"You have to," said Rita briskly as she set the suitcase upright on the porch floor. "We made a deal, remember? Now lift your right leg over and sit down."

"Rita," I said, throwing my leg over her suitcase and sitting, "riding luggage is not going to get me ready to ride Lightning tomorrow. Nothing is going to get me ready to ride Lightning."

Rita pulled out her other suitcase, set it up, and

straddled it herself, facing me. "Do what I do," she ordered. She held imaginary reins out in front of her and made little clicking noises with her tongue. Her heels nudged the sides of the Samsonite. "Let's go, Ginger. Giddyup."

Kari bunched up a couple of pillows and knelt over them on my bed. "Let's go, Rocky!"

"Let's go, Lightning," I mimicked, holding invisible reins, clicking my tongue and my heels. "Let's go, nice and slow."

"See?" said Rita. "What's to be afraid of? Now let's turn the horses. Pull the reins over to the right."

I steered my suitcase to the right. "If only Lightning would shrink to this size by tomorrow morning, I'd be able to do it," I said between tongue clicks.

"Now press your knees in! Squeeze tight! Hold on!" Rita cried. "We're going for a gallop!"

I pressed, I squeezed, I held. We all started galloping on our horses for all we were worth, clicking and shouting.

"Go, Ginger!" Rita cried. "Go, go, go!"

"Go, Rocky!" Kari yelled.

"Go, Lightning!" I cried. "Go, Samsonite!"

"Go crazy!" a voice outside called in.

Rita gave a little shriek as our horses came to a fast halt.

There, silhouetted against the screen door, were the shapes of Sinker and Rusty, laughing like maniacs.

"What do you want?" Kari yelled to them. "If you're sick, go around to the front!"

"You're the sick ones!" said Sinker. "Sick in the head!" He was doubled over, cackling and snorting. "We're . . . supposed to . . . ask you . . . " He gasped for air, "to the campfire . . . tonight."

Rusty caught his breath first. "It's end-of-session campfire," he explained. "Right after dinner. Strays are invited."

"Stray dogs, stray cats, stray crazies," added Sinker.

"We'll think about it," said Rita, tossing her ponytail haughtily.

"We will check our calendars," I said, sticking my nose in the air, "to see if we are free."

"But you must excuse us now," said Kari in the same snooty voice, "because we have got to . . . RIDE!"

And with that the three of us started whooping and yelling, bouncing and jouncing, galloping away on our trusty steeds until we left the intruders far behind, choking in a cloud of dust.

As we got ready for dinner that night, Rita insisted that Kari and I dress up and gleefully decked us out from her own wardrobe. Kari didn't look quite like herself without a flannel shirt. She was wearing a rose-colored jersey with a V neck and little puffed sleeves. Rita had lent me a lavender sweat shirt with lace at the neck and cuffs. But Rita still took the cake in a brilliant pink T-shirt covered in aqua ribbon bows with rhinestone centers.

I was glad we'd dressed up when I got to the Dining Hall and saw that the Scouts were wearing their full uniforms. Tonight Sinker wasn't the only one with a badge sash across his chest. I saw that Hans had so many badges they filled the front of his sash and started going up the back.

As we sat at Doc's table for our last dinner at Ironvale, Rita started in. "Are you getting any badges at campfire tonight, Rusty?" she asked.

"Three," said Rusty. "Art, wood carving, and astronomy."

"Oh, that's wonderful!" gushed Rita. "I just love astronomy. I'm a Taurus."

Rusty started to say something, but Rita had already shifted her gaze one boy to the left. "What about you, Stinker?" she asked. "Are you getting some more badges?"

"Yep," Sinker told us. "I'm getting archery, hiking, music, and bugling, fingerprinting—"

"Fingerprinting?" said Rita. "Like the F.B.I.?"

"Right," said Sinker. "Plus, I got wood carving and beekeeping."

"Beekeeping!" Kari about choked on her bug juice. "I'll tell you one thing, Schwimm. You better keep those bees away from me!"

After dinner Rita actually volunteered to clear. As she reached the kitchen door, I saw Sinker go over and whisper something to her. At first Rita looked puzzled, but then she flashed a big smile.

On the way to the Council Ring for the campfire, Rita walked with Sinker ahead of Kari and me. The two of them kept whispering. At last Rita nodded to Sinker and then turned to us.

"Burrrr!" she said dramatically. "It feels a little chilly tonight. I think I'll go back to the Health Lodge and get a sweater. Meet you at the campfire."

With that she took off.

Kari and I walked on to the Council Ring and sat down, not far from Troop 97.

It was still light out when Shep announced that the evening would begin with troop skits. The first troop, from Kansas City, did an act without much plot but with plenty of whipped cream pies. It got so wild that the skit had to be stopped before it was over.

Rita scooted in on the bench next to me during the middle of the pie throws. She wasn't wearing a sweater.

"Rita," I whispered, "what was all that about, anyway? You and Sinker?"

"You'll see." She gave me one of her famous winks.

The next troop had a boy pretending to give a serious speech on the importance of dental hygiene. He wore a big oversized man's coat, but there was another boy in back of him, hiding inside the coat, and it was the second boy's arms that stuck out through the sleeves. As the first boy delivered the speech, the other boy's hands did things like scratch his head, pull on his ears, pry his mouth open, and pinch his cheeks. The best was when he pulled a giant toothbrush out of the pocket and tried to brush the speaker's teeth!

But the skit that won first prize was by none other than Troop 97. It was called "How We'll Miss Ironvale!" It wasn't about how they would miss camp after they'd gone back home—it was a takeoff on the Miss America Pageant! All the Scouts were dressed in their ideas of girls' bathing suits, which was mainly pillowcases with holes cut out for their heads and arms. They all wore mop wigs. Hans acted as judge, and just as he was about to award first prize to Mac, who was covered with calamine lotion as Miss Poison Ivy, who should enter stage left but Sinker, as the glamorous Miss Snakebite.

Sinker's eyes were smeared with turquoise shadow, his cheeks blushed bright scarlet, and his lips glistened with Icy Peach as he ka-boomed around the other Miss Ironvale contestants wearing a navy blue racing suit and a very familiar purple bikini top! He, too, wore a mop wig, but his was dyed dark and instead of hanging to his shoulders, it was styled in a high ponytail tied with a pink ribbon.

Everyone howled and clapped as Miss Snakebite was crowned with a toilet seat and handed a bouquet of dandelions. Rita clapped longest of all.

"See, Lila," she said proudly, "I knew I'd need all that makeup and stuff!"

Kari and I exchanged glances as Rita clapped away, wondering whether Rita knew that Sinker was imitating her.

"Rita," Kari whispered, "does Sinker remind you of . . . "

"Of anyone in particular?" I chimed in. "Dressed like that?"

Rita gave us a look like she couldn't believe what she was hearing. "You guys!" she said, "Stinker—Miss Ironvale—it's supposed to be *me!*"

"Congratulations," we told her.

"Thank you," said Rita.

There was a pause then as the performing Scouts got back into their uniforms and sat down. Many of them returned wearing Native American head-dresses, some with just a few feathers sticking up in the back and others with feathers all the way around their heads.

The Council Ring grew quiet, and far away I could hear someone running. The footsteps grew louder as a pair of Scouts, dressed as Indian braves and carrying torches, ran into the center of the ring and lit the campfire. In the golden flickering light the circle of Scouts seemed solemn, yet there was something almost mystical about it.

Shep stood up, majestic in a headdress with black and white feathers trailing down his back. He announced the merit badges and presented them. Sinker earned far more badges than any other Scout, plus he had gone from being a Tenderfoot to Second-Class Rank.

"I always knew Sinker was second-class," I whispered.

Kari giggled, but Rita cautioned us with a stern "Shhhh!"

Hans was awarded several badges, too, and he went from being a Star Scout to Life Rank.

"But he'll always be a star to someone I know," whispered Kari, nudging me with her elbow.

"Oh, right," I said, not sure whether she meant to herself or to Rita . . . or to me.

After the badges one of the Scoutmasters led some songs. He started out with "The Bear Went Over the Mountain," but gradually the songs became more serious until they ended with the Ironvale Alma Mater.

> *"Where the crests of Ozark Mountains*
> *Meet the western sky*
> *Lies the camp where Boy Scouts gather*
> *On a hilltop high."*

As the Scouts sang I searched the faces around the Council Ring until I found my father's. He was singing along, and I could tell his whole heart was in it. It seemed like ages ago when he'd bet me "dollars to doughnuts" that at the end of two weeks at Ironvale I wouldn't want to come home.

"When we say farewell to Ironvale
Camping days are o'er
May the joys of newfound comrades
Live forever more."

I figured I owed my dad a whole lot of doughnuts.

The song ended, and everyone was silent as the campfire burned down to embers. I looked up at the night sky, and my eye caught a single bright star flickering.

Star light, star bright,
First star I've seen tonight.
I wish I may, I wish I might
Have the wish I wish tonight.

What should I wish, I wondered? It should be a big wish, an important wish. But before I could decide, several of the Scouts who had earned their astronomy badges stood and took turns pointing out constellations. Rusty showed us how to find the constellation of the Eagle.

"The Eagle's head is made of three stars," he said, and as he described the position of the stars, I began to see the Eagle plainly. It was flying upward with its wings stretched way out. The brightest star in the Eagle's head was the one I had been trying to wish on.

"The most brilliant star in this constellation," Rusty continued, as if knowing my thoughts, "is called Altair."

Altair light, Altair bright, I began again. I wanted to make a stupendous wish on the brightest star in the Eagle. But what? I didn't want to wish I could discover the S.O.S. anymore. And wishing to win races at the swimming meets this summer didn't seem an important enough wish for Altair.

Star light, star bright. Maybe I should wish something about Eagle Peak, wish to figure out all the jumble of things I might have learned up there. Or maybe I should wish something about Hans. But what exactly? I didn't know.

Finally Shep got up and pointed out the constellation of Pegasus, the winged horse.

"From the very beginning of time," he said, "people have wondered at the mysteries of the nighttime heavens, the secrets of the stars. They have seen pictures in star patterns and made up tales about those pictures as a way of explaining the world. As you look up at the sky tonight, you are seeing the same stars that people have gazed at for thousands upon thousands of years."

Shep's voice below and the stars above carried us all back to ancient Greece as he told the myth of Pegasus, the magnificent flying horse. It seems that the horse's rider became so conceited about his ability to ride the great flying horse that he thought he was equal to the gods. He tried to ride Pegasus up to Mount Olympus so he could live with the gods. But the gods didn't like this idea much, so they sent a gadfly to sting Pegasus, and he bucked and bucked and threw his rider, who landed in a patch of thorns and broke both his legs. Pegasus flew on up to the heavens alone where he lives to this day.

I looked at Pegasus for a long time. I could see him kicking wildly in the air, his back arched to throw his rider.

Star light, star bright, I chanted to myself one last time. I squeezed my eyes shut and wished on Altair with all my might that no gadfly would be around tomorrow to sting Lightning.

"Let's go," said Rita brightly after we finished breakfast. She led the way down Red Rock Trail to the stables.

Charlie and Kari were already there. In the riding ring, tethered to a post, was an enormous black-and-white horse. She stomped one hoof, flared her nostrils, and let out a disgusting snuffling sound.

"She doesn't like me," I said.

"She likes you," said Kari.

"I think my scrambled eggs are coming up," I said.

"What are you so afraid of?" asked Kari. "Try to say it."

"Well, for starters," I said, "why is she named Lightning?"

"Just a little joke," explained Charlie. "Her mate's Thunder so we called her Lightning. But they don't make 'em any more slow and gentle than ol' Light here."

I hoped that Charlie spoke the truth.

"One more thing," I said. "Are there any gadflies around here?"

"Gadflies?" Charlie's eyebrows shot up. "All we've got are plain old horseflies and they're nothing to be afraid of."

"But what if one of them bit Lightning and—"

"Lila!" exclaimed Rita. "Forget that story about the Pegasaurus! That was a myth!"

"Okay, okay," I said. "Just checking."

"And the cinch," said Kari, remembering what I'd told her about the belt around my pony's middle on my one and only ride, "is tight as can be. Look."

I looked. "It seems tight," I said, "but it could come loose."

Rita rolled her eyes at Charlie as if to say I was hopeless. I remembered how she'd tried her hardest to learn to swim at Stray Creek. I felt awful and babyish, standing there, whining about getting on this horse.

"It's normal to be afraid the first time," said Charlie in a soothing voice. "Once you get on, you'll be less afraid. You'll see. I've taught hundreds of Scouts to ride, Lila. But I've never had one of 'em yet turn upside down. And I've never had anyone tell me they wish I hadn't helped 'em get up on a horse."

"Just show her who's boss," said Rita again.

"But what if Lightning doesn't know that I'm the boss?" I asked.

"She doesn't know," said Charlie. "It's your job to show her. You just have to get it clear in your mind. That's all. Then she'll know."

I opened my swamp green eyes and stared into the muddy brown eyes of Lightning. *Hey, Lightning? It's me, Lila Fenwick, also known as the Mighty Minnow. Mighty 'cause I'm fast and in charge. In charge, hear that? Don't let my minnow size fool you and I won't let your monster size fool me. I'm talking to you, horse. This is your future rider speaking.*

"Lemme up there!" I called to Charlie.

Charlie put my left foot in the stirrup and gave me a boost up onto the broad and steady back of Lightning. Then he walked around the front of the horse and tucked my right foot into the other stirrup. He did some little adjustment to the strap.

"Give ol' Light a nice pat, Lila," instructed Charlie. "She needs a little love."

"Good Lightning." I patted uncertainly. Lightning blinked a fly out of one eye. She had long straight eyelashes. Her neck felt warm and sleek. I moved my hand over the white hair, over the black. Lightning stood still.

Charlie handed me the reins. I held them while he took the front part of Lightning's bridle and began walking slowly. I felt my left side go up a little and then my right. Left, right. Ka-boom, *boom*. Ka-boom *boom*. It wasn't that bad. Kari was grinning at me with those teeth of hers.

"You're doing just great!" Rita cheered me on. "Fan-tastic!"

I thought about smiling, but not yet. We had walked halfway around the ring. I wasn't upside down.

"How do you feel?" asked Charlie. "Okay?"

I nodded.

"Good ol' Lightning," said Charlie softly. "Light's my girl, light of my life."

Around the ring, all the way around. Then Charlie stopped. "Had enough for one day?" he asked.

Before I had a chance to answer, Rita yelled, "That was only three minutes! You said you'd stay on for five!"

We walked around again. When we got back to where we started, Charlie helped me down. Once on the ground I looked at where I'd been, at that saddle, far above my head. I couldn't believe I'd been up there!

"Here," said Charlie, handing me a little apple. "Give Lightning a treat and thank her for the ride."

Even though I'd survived my five minutes on top of Lightning, I wasn't sure I wanted anything to do with the rest of her. Especially with her teeth. I held the apple in my outstretched palm and slowly extended it to Lightning. She plucked up the apple with her velvety lips, barely tickling my palm.

"Thanks, Lightning," I whispered. I patted her on the neck a few more times while I thanked my lucky

Altair that no gadflies had shown up. Lightning nodded her head and gave a soft whinny.

"Thank you, too, Charlie," I said ducking under the wooden fence. Rita and Kari dashed up and hugged me as if I'd just won the Olympic jumping medal.

"It's a start!" said Kari. "You liked it, right? Admit it. It was fun being up there on Lightning. Next summer you'll really get the hang of it and we'll all go riding. Every day!"

Next summer. I looked at Rita and Kari and thought about next summer. And right then and there I knew when I saw Altair again, I'd have a wish all ready.

After my ride Rita and I went back to the Health Lodge while Kari stayed at the stable to groom Rocky.

Rita heaved her suitcases onto her bunk and sighed. "It's unreal that this is over," she said. "I wish we could stick around all summer, like Kari."

"Me too," I said, looking out through the screens of the porch. Lots of Scouts were leading their parents around the camp to show them everything they'd been doing for the past two weeks. I wondered how many of them had spent the night on Eagle Peak. I wondered what they'd discovered.

Just as I finished stuffing my clothes into the duffel bag, I heard two sets of Samsonite locks click into place. I knew it was time to go.

Kari came back from the stable just in time to help

roll one of the Samsonite twins up to the parking lot. There we found my mom and dad talking to Shep Dorty. All our stuff was sitting in neat little piles surrounding the open trunk of our car.

"Here they come now," said my dad, pointing to the three of us. "Now that you see them, you still want to take the bet?"

"What bet did you make about us?" I asked.

But Shep wasn't looking at us. He seemed to be zeroing in on Rita's suitcases.

"You're on," said Shep. With that he hoisted the largest Samsonite into the trunk and began positioning things around it.

"Shep bet us that he could pack the trunk with both suitcases," explained my dad, "and all the rest of our gear."

We watched for a few seconds as Shep rearranged suitcases, sleeping bags, and backpacks in the trunk.

Suddenly Rita began waving madly to some khaki blurs all the way across the Parade Grounds. "Hi, Rusty! Hi, Stinker! Hi, Hans!"

Boy did she ever have eagle eyes!

Rita kept waving as the three blurs cut across the field and headed in our direction.

"Hey," said Hans, coming into focus as he approached our car. "Going back to civilization?"

"Lila and I *have* to go back." Rita sighed. "But Kari's so lucky! She gets to stay here for the rest of the summer. I wish I could stay too," she added, giving one of her meaningful looks at Hans.

I just kept quiet, but Hans looked at me anyway.

"You going back to help out the swim team at N.A.P.?" Hans asked.

"I guess," I told him.

"I think they can use your help," Hans said. "I got a letter from Michael a couple days ago, and he said N.A.P. hasn't won a single race in a meet yet."

"You're kidding!" I said. "Not even Kelly?"

"I told you it's a sleepy team." He gave one of his crookedest smiles. "You know, you really should swim for Shaw Park." I must have given him a funny look, because he said, "I mean it. I saw you swim that day at N.A.P. You're good enough to make the team."

"I don't know," I said, flattered out of my mind. "I thought you had to be twelve to swim for Shaw Park."

"You do," said Hans. "You're twelve, aren't you?"

"Not quite," I said.

"Oh," said Hans. "Well, maybe next year. I thought you were older."

"You thought I was *older?*" I couldn't believe my ears. "But that day—when you came to N.A.P. with Michael? You got me mixed up with Jimmy Jansey's sister, who just got out of third grade!"

Hans looked puzzled. "Third grade?" He frowned. "Not the sister I'm thinking of."

"You mean . . . he's got another sister?" I asked.

"He's got four," Hans said. "Anyway, you should

think about swimming for Shaw Park when you do turn twelve."

I was trying to let all this sink in when Rita announced, "I'm turning twelve next month. Maybe I could swim for Shaw Park. Or do you have to wear those hideous tank suits?"

"There!" Shep Dorty exclaimed, breathing heavily. "It's all in."

We turned and saw that there were no more piles scattered around the car. Shep had, it seemed, managed to wedge every single item into our trunk.

"It's all in," said my dad, "but the lid's not shut yet. That's the true test."

Shep tried one slam by himself. When that didn't work he called, "Pearson! Schwimm! Hart! You're recruited for trunk duty!" Rusty and Sinker stood on either side of the trunk, Hans and Shep by the back. On the count of three they all shoved down as hard as they could. The trunk closed. I wondered if we'd ever get it open.

"Well," said my dad, looking stunned that someone had packed a tighter trunk than he had, "you did it." He kept shaking his head. "We don't know how, but you did it."

My dad put his hand to his neckerchief then and slowly pulled off the giant orange lobster claw that held it in place. He handed the claw to Shep. "Take good care of it," he cautioned. "We made it the summer of the jamboree in California. Remember?"

Shep nodded. "Don't worry, Phil. I'll give you a chance to win it back next summer."

"Next summer?" I said, turning to my father. "You're going to be camp doctor again?"

"Yep," he said. "We think we should make it a tradition, don't you, girls?"

"Yes!" shouted Rita.

"Well, we gotta get going," said Sinker. "We have to pick up our wood carving projects."

"Bye!" Rita called as the Scouts walked away. "Hey! I know! We'll write to you guys!"

After the boys left I looked around for Kari, but she wasn't there. Rita noticed she was missing the same time I did.

"She probably hates good-byes," I said. I couldn't exactly blame her, but still I felt sort of cheated, her disappearing like that.

My mom was already in the car. Rita, my dad, and I climbed in, too, and we pulled out of the Camp Ironvale parking lot. We were waving to Shep and Mrs. Lindquist as my parents began singing:

"The ants go marching one by one, hurrah! Hurrah!
The ants go marching one by one, hurrah! Hurrah!"

Suddenly a sound of hoof beats clattered above the song and above engine noise. When we looked out the window, there was Kari, galloping on Rocky along the trail beside the road, waving and waving. We rolled down the window, waving like mad, and sang out at the top of our lungs:

"The ants go marching one by one,
The little one stops to shoot the gun
And they all go marching . . ."

It was as if those two weeks at Boy Scout camp had never happened. At least that's how it felt sometimes, as I sat on my towel behind the diving board at N.A.P. listening to Kelly read from her sister's magazine and watching Michael doing his pushup routine. But when I looked over at the towel next to mine and saw Rita Morgan in a navy blue tank suit, I knew something had happened.

We'd been back from Ironvale for two weeks. Coach had given Rita a swimming lesson every day since we'd been back, and while she wasn't ready to swim in the meets, she was making great progress. I still couldn't believe my eyes sometimes when I saw her in the shallow end of the pool, dog-paddling furiously from side to side, her ponytail a wet sausage clinging to the back of her neck.

Today as I listened to Kelly, I kept a sharp eye out for Gayle. She'd called last night, the minute she'd gotten back from fat camp, and had been very mysterious when I asked her whether she'd changed or not.

"You'll just have to wait and decide for yourself when you see me tomorrow," she'd said. "Sometimes I think I have and other times I think I haven't."

The article Kelly was reading to Rita and me was called "The Secrets of the Stars."

" 'TV star Alexis LaMont puts sliced cucumber circles over her eyes when they feel tired and puffy,' " read Kelly. " ' "It gives me more energy on the set," ' says Alexis, "and changes my whole outlook on life." ' "

I cracked up. "I guess putting cucumbers on your eyes would change your outlook! Maybe she should try slices of cantaloupe! That would really change her outlook!"

"Shhh!" Rita gave me a look. "You know, you could have puffy eyes some day."

"It's not one of my major worries at the moment," I told her.

Listening to the Great Advice of Alexis LaMont had almost made me miss the white terry cloth-robed figure walking down the steps from the girls' locker room.

"Gayle!" I jumped up and ran to meet her, getting a whistle from the lifeguard.

"No running!" he shouted.

"Okay! Okay!" I shouted back. But I kept running until I collided with Gayle in a giant hug. "Gayle! You do feel thinner!" I said, and she did.

"My clothes are all too big," she told me as we began walking slowly toward the shade behind the diving board, "so I know I must look different. But I don't feel any different. Does that make sense?"

"I guess," I said.

"Hi, Gayle!" called Kelly as we approached the towels.

Gayle gave me a what's-going-on look as she saw Rita stretched out on a hot pink towel next to Kelly.

"Welcome back, Gayle!" Rita sounded as if she and Gayle were lifelong friends. "Hey! Even in that beach robe, I can tell you're not so fat anymore!"

I froze. No one ever called Gayle fat. Not *ever!* Slowly Gayle turned toward Rita and gave her a look that would have made most people crawl under the nearest towel. But not Rita. She stood up and circled around Gayle.

"Your cheeks aren't all puffed out like they were," Rita went on. "And your double chin's gone! You look terrific! Let's see the rest."

Gayle smiled an odd smile, tossing her head and whipping her long hair very close to Rita's face, and then went into an imitation of a high fashion model, doing turns and opening her robe in quick flashes, giving glimpses of a new tank suit and a new shape.

"You could be dynamite!" Rita stood with her hands on her hips. "You've got to get all new clothes, right? You are soooo lucky! I could help you shop. And you've *got* to stop wearing that ratty old robe!"

It seemed that Rita had plenty of Great Advice for Gayle in the S.O.S.—the Secrets of Style!

Before Gayle could say a word to Rita, Coach's whistle blew for the start of afternoon practice. We all headed for the pool. Gayle walked next to me, stuffing her hair into her racing cap. "I'm not the only thing around here that's different," she remarked.

"If you mean Rita," I said, "she's really not that bad, once you know how to take her."

"It's hard to believe," said Gayle. "And something seems different about you too."

"It does?" I asked. "What?"

Gayle shook her head. "I don't know exactly. Just something."

"Backstrokers into the water!" Coach called.

"Something good?" I asked her as I lowered myself into the shallow end of the pool and took hold of the handles on the starting blocks.

"Something . . . interesting!" called Gayle.

I pressed my feet against the side of the pool and coiled my body up tight against my knees.

"Take your mark! Get set . . . GO!"

I lunged backward, shoving off hard with my feet, and let the glide take me as far it could. Then with steady even strokes I pulled toward the far end of the pool, not feeling at all like the Mighty Minnow.

About the Author

Kate McMullan grew up in St. Louis, Missouri, and was graduated from the University of Tulsa in Oklahoma. In addition to her first novel, *The Great Ideas of Lila Fenwick*, Ms. McMullan is the coauthor, with Lisa Eisenberg, of a number of puzzle books including *Fishy Riddles, Buggy Riddles*, and the soon to be published *Grizzly Riddles* (all Dial). Ms. McMullan lives with her husband, artist James McMullan, and their daughter in New York City and in Sag Harbor, Long Island.